4.24

A DATE & A TIME

Navid Daffuwala

Ukiyoto Publishing

All global publishing rights are held by

Ukiyoto Publishing

Published in 2024

Content Copyright © Navid Daffuwala

ISBN 9789364942423

All rights reserved.

No part of this publication may be reproduced, transmitted, or stored in a retrieval system, in any form by any means, electronic, mechanical, photocopying, recording or otherwise, without the prior permission of the publisher.

The moral rights of the author have been asserted.

This is a work of fiction. Names, characters, businesses, places, events, locales, and incidents are either the products of the author's imagination or used in a fictitious manner. Any resemblance to actual persons, living or dead, or actual events is purely coincidental.

This book is sold subject to the condition that it shall not by way of trade or otherwise, be lent, resold, hired out or otherwise circulated, without the publisher's prior consent, in any form of binding or cover other than that in which it is published.

www.ukiyoto.com

Dear Reader,

The story is fictional, but the emotions are true. There are still so many rape cases which are open and actual rapists are yet to be get punishments. Wish there will be a person who will help their families to take out of it and give justice to their daughter, wife, sister, and mother.

This includes some scenes which are cruel and based on real scenarios which may or may not be known. If you are not looking for a detailing of rape or punishments, then you can close the book right now. But believe me, you will not regret it after reading the story and plot.

CONTENTS

Chapter 1	5
Chapter 2	37
Chapter 3	73
Chapter 4	111
Chapter 5	149

New Delhi. 24th April 2017

It was Four O'clock in the mornings. At a farmhouse away from the city, a girl was screaming. She was screaming so loud and asking for help. But the place was so far from the city that no one could hear her voice. Her clothes were torn from chest, thighs, and shoulders. She was having so many scratches on her body and blood was falling. Her eyes were red, and her body was shivering. She was crying and running from someone. That someone was none other than Mr. Luthra.

***

Mr. Luthra was 57-year-old businessman, and everyone knows him. For so many people, he was a god father. He was an inspiration and has charitable trust for orphanages, appeared in big magazines and has a small family with a wife and two children. His name was in the Top Three Businessman's list. After so many years of hard work, he earned money and power to control the whole country.

***

Mr. Luthra: Come on. Why are you running from me? There is nowhere you can go. I bought this big farmhouse just for us. Don't run so much. I am too old anyway for this. You are making me use all my energy in running. What will we do in bed? Huh?

Mr. Luthra was trying to rape her. She arrived at the door and started knocking on it, screaming loudly for help.

Girl: No. Please, help. Somebody, open the door. Please let me out. Is somebody out there? Please help open it. I want to go.

She was breathing heavily, screaming so loud and crying for help, unfortunately, nobody was there to listen. Mr. Luthra came after her. He felt breathlessness. He took a deep breath, cracked his back a little and started walking towards her.

Mr. Luthra: As I told you darling, nobody is here to hear your scream. I am not going to hurt you. Although, I will give you lots of money to enjoy the rest of your life. In return, all I want is your virginity. At first, it hurts but it is a lot of fun later.

He forcibly grabbed her hand and started pounding her. She was trying extremely hard to stop him, but she was not strong enough to resist. Mr. Luthra slammed her at the door, turned over forcibly and started ripping off her clothes again.

Girl: Please, stop. I am just sixteen. Let me go.

Mr. Luthra: Oh, stop shouting. Just enjoy it. I know you are just sixteen, that is why I want you. I am not going to hurt you, darling. Just a few minutes and you will be holy.

Suddenly, he heard someone walking quietly and the smell of a dirty sock. As soon as he turned around to look, someone cut his throat slightly. He was wearing a formal black suit, and his entire face was covered with a black mask. Mr. Luthra is not able to say anything, but he is alive. He fell on the ground. That person saw a girl crying and pointed at room, as telling her to leave from there. She grabbed her torn clothes from the ground and ran towards the room without looking back and wondering what that person would do with Mr. Luthra.

**

There were paintings on the wall and a flowerpot with fake flowers on the table. Mr. Luthra grabbed those things and started throwing them at people.

That person first dodged and strongly grabbed his left hand to again make a long cut on his forearms. He started crying and trying to speak but could not. His right hand is on his throat which is stopping blood and left hand is pouring blood constantly which he can't stop. Because of the cut, his second hand loses sensation and muscles being weak. After a few minutes, his left arm became paralyzed. A person is standing there without saying a word or any other intense movement.

Mr. Luthra tried to open the door, but it was locked from the outside. He started running away from him. Again, that person stabbed the knee of left leg. Mr. Luthra fell to the ground. He tried to walk again but it was so intense that his leg was paralyzed too in no time. That person did not get closer to Mr. Luthra till that time. When all this was done, he opened the droor and found magazines and newspapers which had his photo on the front page. The person tore only those pages that contained his face and spread all around. Mr. Luthra tries to fold his hands and begs for his life. Person was waiting until all the blood comes out from his body, and he died. Blood flow was too much and in no time, Mr. Luthra died. The time was 4:24 in the morning on the date of 24th April. This whole incident took only 20 minutes.

∗∗

Person was standing there for a few minutes after his death. Suddenly, the police siren heard. Police opened the door and saw Mr. Luthra dead, and that person was standing there. Police pointed guns at the murderer and asked him to remove the mask and surrender. A person removed the mask, and everybody was shocked.

Chapter 1

Things were started or ended way before,
But we always realize lately.

4.24 - A Date & A Time

2 years Ago.
New Delhi. 24ᵗʰ April 2015

Two little girls are running in an empty garden. Laughing, playing, jiggling with mother and father. Family was so joyful and playing with a ball.
Mother: Inayat, catch it. Throw it to Abbu.
Father: Yay! My brave girl. Now, go there and I will throw it towards you. Hold your sister's hand and take her with you too.
It was a dream and unfortunately, someone shouted loudly from downstairs.
Fatima: Anaya? Anaya? You got a call from work. Where is your mobile? Come downstairs, it's urgent.

***

Anaya was a Muslim girl living in New Delhi. She graduated in Forensic Medicine and was a gold medalist. She had been working in Delhi Crime Branch for a very long time. She was working on a drug case in which she had to postmortem and examine three bodies.

***

Anaya's house has a Muslim feature as, a hall on the ground floor where "la ilaha illallah muhammadur rasulullah" is written in Urdu in a frame. There was a at 6AM and azaan can be heard from nearer masjid. Sofa with chairs places in hall and Makkah painting hanging on a wall. The Quran was placed on a table near to the sofa. Fatima, who is Anaya's mother was shouting from the ground floor. Anaya was sleeping on the first floor. Her room is Green and Cream color with lots of books in a shelf. A painting with two girls playing in a park is hanging on the face side of the wall. Her mobile lightens up and has 12 missed calls and 4 messages from Shekhar. Her bed is scatter and she is sleeping wearing Kurta and Jeans. A white cat is sleeping beside her.

Fatima: Anaya? Anaya? Where is your phone. There is a call for you. Come downstairs.

Anaya felt annoyed, took the second pillow beside her and covered her ears. A cat came to her and started ponding her. Anaya removed the pillow and started petting her. Her mother was shouting constantly.

Anaya: Coming Ammi.

Anaya came downstairs with an irritated face.

Anaya: I want to sleep more. I want to sleep just a little bit more. Who is calling Ammi?

Fatima: I know beta, but it is your job, your duty to the world. It is Shekhar. Your junior. He said it is urgent.

She snatched the phone from his mother's hand.

Anaya: What now?

Shekhar: Murder took place in Orange Farmhouse. The victim's name is Mr. Bose, that rich businessperson with lots of hotels, cruises, casinos, and all. I was thinking it is a money matter.

Anaya: Shekhar, stop assuming those things. That is not our job to assume why he got murdered. What do the police say?

After listening to this, Fatima turned on the TV to see the news. Shekhar was talking continuously, but her ears only listened to the voice of reporter in the TV.

Reporter: Everyone is shocked on Mr. Bose's death at his own farmhouse. Who murdered Mr. Bose? Is it about money? Recently he appeared in the top 25 richest person magazine.

Anaya snatched remote from mother's hand and turned it off. She covers mobile with hand.

Anaya: Don't watch TV in the morning. Go and read the Quran and Namaz.

Shekhar (Continues): They want us to be at the crime scene right now. I am going there, and I will share you the address. I know you haven't slept for the past few hours but, please be there.

Anaya: Oh god. It is not a few, it is more than two days. Why did I choose forensics? Anyway, I will be there in a few minutes.

She hung up the call irritably, and as soon as she turned around, her mother was staring at her. Anaya went to her room upstairs and grabbed her phone and vehicle keys.

Fatima: Again?

Anaya: Yes. Again. Someone murdered Mr. Bose, and I am going to the Farmhouse. Don't know when I will return so don't wait for me for namaz, lunch or dinner. Take care. Khuda hafiz Ammi.

Her mother grabbed her hand and tied it up to a black thread without saying anything and kissed her on her forehead.

Fatima: Don't take too much stress for anything. Remember, you are not responsible for anything happening in your life. You are not doing anything wrong. Allah will always be there to protect you. I know this will happen so, I packed breakfast for you and Shekhar. Khuda hafiz.

Anaya left at the crime scene.

**

Anaya arrives at the crime scene in a car. Everything is sealed with a crime scene tape. She confirms her identity at the gate. A cameraman recording. A reporter is speaking in front of a camera. Three constables Infront of barricades outside farmhouse, two constables stopping reporters.

Anaya: So, have you got anything?

Shekhar: Glass with lipstick is what we have. The team is trying to find more evidence.

Anaya started her work with Shekhar and team to collect evidence. That crime scene was under Inspector Manoj, and he enter in the farmhouse.

***

Manoj was a one of the best Police Inspectors in state. He received medals, trophies, transfers for killing big mafias and stopped illegal businesses, selling drugs, raids and much more. Somehow, more than one year back he lost the love of his life in a car accident, and it changed a lot. He was enthusiastic about his work but after that incident, he felt like he didn't want to do anything for his life. He doesn't want to live. His parents were dead in childhood and lived alone after that. After more than a one year, this was his first case he received.

***

Manoj: Ms. Anaya, have you got any clue?

Anaya: Sir, my team is collecting and trying to get as most of the evidence. He is my colleague, Shekhar.

Shekhar is working but listening to their conversation. He stands up and joins them.

Shekhar: Actually, I am her junior. We were once studying in same college, but…

Anaya interrupted him.

Anaya: Okay. Once we find anything, we will check and diagnose the body and share the reports with you. Have you got any clues who did this and why?

Manoj: We haven't found anything yet. It is private property so there is no CCTV, no security guard was there when it took place, nothing. His family did not even know where he was last night. They said last night they were at a party and then he left without saying anything. His family was curious and reported a missing case a few hours back. He was a businessman, so we thought maybe he went at meeting or something.

**

After searching places when we reached here, we found his body hanging with a fan. We found that he was not alone. There was someone else in this room with him because we found nail scratches and lipstick on glass.

Anaya: Is it about money or personal? Anything like that? Although, he is one of the richest people in the state.

Shekhar: Now who is judging?

Manoj: Not yet. We are into it. You start your work and let me know if you get any clue.

4.24 - A Date & A Time

Manoj leaves with his team to police station. Media started following and shouting. Two men from his team were searching outside of farmhouse road for footstep.

Shekhar and Anaya continue their work. They collect two vine glasses, rope, skin and hair samples, small part of ripped clothes on a door handle.

**

Anaya and Shekhar arrive at the lab with evidence and a dead body. The lab has so much equipment with chemicals. Three man is working with flask and Two woman is working on microscope. Anaya and Shekhar enter Anaya's cabin.

Shekhar: We got so many clues for this. By the way, what about the previous drug case? Is it closed?

Anaya: Not yet. We haven't figured out what drug it was. I sent it for examination and reports will arrive in a few more days.

Anaya: Aren't you at home last night? Or did you sleep here in the lab?

Shekhar: I slept here in lab. You know our work. Even my whole family is in Bhopal, and nobody is waiting at home for me. You must go home once in twenty-four hours or need to call at least because you live in the same city. Your mother will be worried about you.

Anaya: If I go home daily, they will still worry about me. Ammi will say 'Oh, Anaya. Is everything okay? Why would you come early?' And if I don't go home in two days Ammi will say 'Where is my daughter? Is everything okay?'. Oh, she packed an omelet, bread, and boiled eggs for you.

Shekhar: Oh, Great. That is called mother's love. I am so hungry. Say thanks to aunty. Oh, say Shukriya.

Anaya: Surely. You eat and I'll start examining these things.

Anaya started her work and after eating food, Shekhar joined too. They both wear rubber gloves and begin to investigate the evidence they have gotten thoroughly. They started with photographs and glasses of vine.

Anaya: It seems like a girl was with him last night. Do you know about Mr. Bose's nature?

Shekhar: He is 55 years old. I never heard any rumor with a girl or drugs or any other illegal businesses. Although, if he does that and someone even tried to case a file. But because of so much power and money, he closed the case on the spot. Maybe that is why we never heard about it. What we got else?

Anaya: Someone has so much money doesn't mean he or she can commit a crime and hide it with money. Maybe we did not hear about it means he never done such things too.

Shekhar: Okay, ma'am. That can be true too. We got long hair and its smoothness, root sheath, and smells. There was a girl last night. Also, we have ripped cloth part on door with few blood drops on it, and it smells like a lady's perfume. Also, it smells something else too. Can you please check?

Anaya: Yes. It smells like a drug. Doesn't it smell like cocaine to you? Or similar drug. I heard that Mr. Bose was a pure and holy person.

Shekhar: But I don't think they took drugs. I told you earlier, money is power. Once, there were news that

Mr. Bose caught in a rave party with some foreigners. Later, the court declared that Mr. Bose was not guilty, which is proven with sampling.

Anaya: Means he never done that thing. But still, it feels like something is wrong. Ask the team to examine the blood on the cloth and we will check the body.

**

Anaya and Shekhar went to cold storage to investigate Mr. Bose's dead body. Shekhar opened the door where Mr. Bose's body.

Shekhar: So, there are nail scratch marks on his neck, back and chest. Something intense must have happened between both. Because of hanging, there are marks on his neck. Muscles are weak, blood has dried up almost six hours past, and the asphyxiation will cause capillaries in the eyes, neck, and lungs to burst which cause the eyes to become red, foam at mouth. Nothing here.

Anaya: So, he hanged himself then why there was so many scratches? Shekhar, have you noticed it? There are some cuts below his belly. Remove the cloth, please.

Shekhar removed cloth and made the body naked. They see his private part cut in half. They both are shocked, scared and step aside from the body. They breathe heavily and start sweating. Anaya felt vomiting and turned around.

Shekhar: What is this? What kind of death is this? Someone naked him, cut his thing in half! But We did not find any blood in his pants or clothes. What does it mean? After blood dried, he wears his pants again. I am so confused, scared, stressed, and feel like vomiting.

Anaya: It clearly states that it is an intense murder. Call Manoj and tell him to come here immediately. We never faced this kind of case.

Shekhar called Manoj and told him to come to the lab.

**

Manoj and Santosh arrived at the cold storage. Anaya and Shekhar were standing outside of the cold storage, and both were stunned. Anaya informed about the situation to them. Santosh could not hold and went from there.

Manoj: But when we reached there, he was hanging with a fan. I checked whether someone killed him but there is no clue of murder. Nothing. Rope knots, muscles, eyes looked like he hung by himself. Also, there is no blood in his either body or room. Blood dried as usual. I believe that some woman will be there, but how...

Anaya: Mr. Bose hung by himself; we thought the same. We got cloth, hair, and scratches on the dead body. There should be a girl. Have you got any complain against Mr. Bose or someone is missing in last Twelve hours?

Manoj: We talked with his family about the party, and who was present there. We are trying to find clues to the same, but still nothing is in our hand. We haven't received such a complaint yet and my team are also searching for Mr. Bose's house, offices, nearer area wherever he can go or had connections.

4.24 - A Date & A Time

Manoj, Anaya and Shekhar went inside the cold storage. Shekhar looked at Manoj and removed the cloth. Anaya could not stand and turned around, Manoj looked at Mr. Bose's body and got stunned. All of a sudden, Manoj got a call from his police station. They got out from cold storage and Manoj picked up the call.

Police Constable: Sir, we received a missing complaint of a sixteen-year-old girl named Kavya Khanna. Last time she was with his family at the same farmhouse where Mr. Bose. We checked and they all are at the same party as Mr. Bose.

Manoj: What is her parents name? How she looks like? What kind of cloth she wore? Send an image to my phone immediately.

Anaya: What happened?

Manoj: A sixteen-year-old girl is missing. Mr. Bose and that girl with family both were at the same party.

Manoj received a girl image and a message. It mentioned that; 'Girl name is Kavya Khanna and has dark brown hair. Last time she wore a cherry red dress and red lipstick.'

Shekhar: Cherry red dress? Brown hair? We found ripped cloth was also cherry red, and hair color is almost same. Mr. Bose should be with that girl. We must find out where she is! She is the key suspect of this crime.

Manoj called his team and order them to find that girl near the farmhouse.

Shekhar: She is the key to getting near to the murderer. I pray to God that we find that girl as soon as possible.

Manoj and Santosh left to search for Kavya.

Santosh: Sir, you said that the murderer cut his… you know, his… it means, maybe, maybe he is trying to rape that girl, and she did this for self-defense!

Manoj: Don't know Santosh. Maybe or maybe not. Maybe that girl is not the murderer or maybe there was someone else in the room. Maybe the girl who Mr. Bose bought, took or kidnapped whatever it was, she was the in the plan of murdering Mr. Bose. There are thousands of assumptions. First, we need to find that girl.

**

Anaya and Shekhar were working in their lab. Anaya's phone rang and it was Manoj.

Anaya: Hello, yes sir.

Manoj: We found Kavya. Our team found her in the jungle near the farmhouse. Her condition is not good, but you can take the samples from her body.

Anaya: Where is she?

Manoj: In my police station.

**

Anaya and Shekhar went to the police station. Two people are sitting with the constable to file a complaint at two different tables. One constable is arranging files. Two people are sitting on a chair and waiting for their turn. One drunk criminal with a handcuff. Anaya and Shekhar were stunned after seeing Kavya. Dust stuck on Kavya's body, wearing a sheet, and sitting on bench and sobbing. She has a scratch on her body, and the doctor is attending.

Anaya: What happened? Why is she like that?

Manoj: She is not in stage of any clarification. Let her clean up and then we will talk to her. We also informed her parents; they will come here anytime.

Anaya went to Kavya. She asked the doctor to move and started cleaning dust and blood by herself. She applied alcohol to her scratches, and it hurt her.

Anaya: Oh, sorry. Are you okay?

Kavya did not say anything and sobbed continuously. Her parents came. They both went to Kavya.

Mr. Khanna: What happened Manoj? What happened to my daughter? What has caused this condition? Have you found anyone? I need an answer.

***

Mr. Khanna is one of the richest businesspeople and Mr. Bose's professional friend. He and Mr. Bose both are competitors, but they were most likely to be friends. Both have the same numbers of hotels, bars, villas but still Mr. Bose was ahead. There was no jealousy between them. He did not get some news about Mr. Bose's death till now. After Mr. Bose's death, He will be the number one in the city and state.

***

Manoj: Sir, please relax. We are working on it. We will find that person very soon.

Mr. Khanna: What do you mean you still haven't got him? Do something. If you need permission to do anything, then I will provide it for you. I will talk to your seniors. Just find that scoundrel as soon as possible. And I need him alive. If you need power I will give you, if you need money I'll give. But if you can't find him then you don't know what I can do.

As a parent, he was curious for his daughter. Manoj was listening without reacting what he says.

Manoj: Sir, please calm down. My team is already working, and we got so many clues. We want to ask you some questions. Please get in and cooperate.

Mr. Khanna: Why me? Get that scoundrel who has done this to my daughter. And what have you got? His fingerprints? His name? His address? Anything?

Manoj: I will let you know. Please come to the investigation room. Santosh, please bring two glasses of water and tea. What will you have, tea or a coffee?

Mr. Khanna: Is this time to discuss tea or coffee I want? Is this more important to decide what to drink rather than catch that person who did this to my daughter?

Manoj: I will tell you everything. Please come to the investigation room. Santosh, tea for me and a coffee for sir.

Mr. Khanna walked into the investigation room so angrily. Manoj and Santosh entered too.

**

There are four yellow halogen lights at each corner and a table in the center with white light on the top. There are three chairs: two and one side of the table.

Manoj: Please sir, take a seat. Take water.

Mr. Khanna drinks water so angrily.

Mr. Khanna: Now, finish it quickly. I want to be with my daughter.

Manoj: Sure. How do you know Mr. Bose? What is your relationship with him? And what were you doing at his party last night?

Mr. Khanna: Why are you asking such kind of questions? What did this have to do with what happened to my daughter?

Manoj: We found Mr. Bose's dead body at his farmhouse. We also found ripped cloth similar to your daughter's, lipstick, hair and more there. We will interrogate your daughter about that after she feel safe about that incidence. And has your daughter ever taken drugs?

Mr. Khanna got so angry on it, stand from chair, and started shouting.

Mr. Khanna: Do you know what you are doing? What and to whom do you ask these questions? Are you out of your mind? You don't know me and my power. I can terminate or transfer you in just one minute.

Manoj could not stand any more, and he slapped hard to Mr. Khanna.

Manoj: Situation is, I am so calm person. But, because of people like you, I forget my calmness. I am saying continuously 'Please calm down, please cooperate' but you did not listen. Now, please be patient and answer only those questions I am asking. And if you say something other than this, then you know what I can do. Is it okay, Mr. Khanna?

Mr. Khanna covered his cheek with hand, nodded his head and sat on a chair again. A child who was working on a tea stall came with tea and a coffee. Manoj asked him to serve Mr. Khanna first.

Mr. Khanna: We both are businesspeople, that is why I know him. Also, we were good friends. I had several deals with him in the past. Mr. Luthra organized yesterday's success party. His name came in the Top Ten richest businessperson. I don't know him very well, but he is a businessperson like us, so we knew him. We met several times at parties or special occasions. As for my daughter, she never did drugs. Yesterday evening, Mr. Bose said he got an offer to buy a hotel. After a few minutes, he left to deal for the hotel. But this does not mean he kidnapped my daughter. I have known Mr. Bose for so many years. He is old, straight minded, and cheerful person. He had a family; wife, children so, he will never do that.

Manoj: We can't say anything right now. But thanks for the information. Please sit outside, we will ask some questions to your daughter. And yes. I am genuinely sorry for that slap. I respect you but, in my territory please cooperate.

Mr. Khanna nodded his head. He stands and leaves outside of the room.

Manoj: Santosh? What about Kavya? Is she okay?

Santosh: No sir. He is still crying and sobbing. Doctor Anaya is cleaning her wounds.

Manoj: She is not a doctor. Forget it. Ask Anaya if we can interrogate Kavya or not? I think she will handle her.

Santosh goes outside and sees Anaya pampering Kavya. Santosh asked by nodding his head. Anaya looked at Kavya and held her both shoulders. Kavya understood and stood up and walked towards Santosh. Anaya also walked with her while holding her shoulder.

**

Kavya sat on a bench. Manoj offered a glass of water to Kavya.

Manoj: Don't be scared. We are here to help you. Drink this. Tell me what happened to you. What happened last night?

Kavya could not say anything. She was scared and sobbing while drinking water. She did not even look up at anyone.

Anaya: Can't we do this later? She is scared about yesterday's incident.

Manoj: Yes, you are right. Santosh…

Kavya interrupts her started giving her statement.

Kavya: I was at the party with my mother and father. They knew them so I stayed with my parents. I was with my father while he was with his friends. Then, he introduced me to Mr. Bose. At first, he was a gentleman but, later he started teasing me, touching me on shoulders, waist and slowly to chest.

Kavya felt breathless and started crying. Anaya gave her water and calmed her down.

Manoj: What was your parents were doing?

Kavya: Mom was with some aunties and father was talking with other people. I am too much connected with my dad so, I was with father. We sat at the table. Mr. Bose came and sat beside me. After some time, he started touching me on my thighs. He was the worst person I ever met.

Kavya cried continuously and she held her head tight in stress. Anaya tries to keep her calm down.

Manoj: Anaya, please take her out. We will take her statement after she feels good.

Anaya nodded his head and grabbed Kavya's shoulder to pick her up, but Kavya continued.
Kavya: Then, I drank orange juice, and I blacked out.
Anaya: Orange juice? Who gave it to you?
Kavya: Waiter was passing, and I took it, nothing else. But, after a few minutes I fell asleep, and I woke up with torn clothes at farmhouse. I was not sure at first, but it was Mr. Bose's farmhouse. My head felt very heavy, looked blurry and I saw him taking cocaine.
Manoj brought the evidence they found. He took a torn cloth in a bag and placed Infront of Kavya.
Manoj: Is it yours?
Kavya nodded her head.
Anaya: He also forced you for cocaine, that is why your clothes smell like that, right?
Kavya: Yes. He forced me to take that because he wanted to rape me. After cocaine, he became so strong and tried to rip my clothes off, hurting me with his nails, and…
Kavya started crying while memorizing all those things. Anaya calmed her down and tried to take her out, but she wanted to give her statement.
Kavya: I tried to stop him as I can. I tried to push him away, scratch his body to hurt him, but he was so strong that I could not. Suddenly someone came wearing a black formal suit and black mask and hit a flowerpot on his head. His body was fully covered so I could not see him. He signaled me to go out. What happened after that, I don't know. I went out and hid and I was waiting for someone to come from the main road. When I heard the police siren, I came out.

4.24 - A Date & A Time

Kavya's statement completed. She stood by herself, and Anaya took her outside to her parents.

**

Manoj asks Santosh to bring Mr. Khanna again.

Manoj: Please sit sir. Anaya will take care of your daughter. After Kavya's statement, Kavya needs to be checked fully. If anything happened to her or not. Please cooperate.

Mr. Khanna: Okay Inspector. But we both will be there.

Anaya took Kavya to her lab and started to examine her. She found blood and drugs on her body which was related to Mr. Bose's. During the investigation, they found hair which was different from Kavya's DNA as well as Mr. Bose's.

Anaya: Is there anyone else with you two there?

Kavya: I blacked out after drinking that juice. When I woke up, there were we only two. I don't have any idea what happened between that time.

Anaya took her mobile, called Manoj and informed about it.

Shekhar: It is murderer's hair, or we can say savior. Whoever he is, he is very clever. He did not leave any hole in his work, but at least we got a hair.

Anaya: But check it closely. It doesn't feel a men's hair from smoothness and tissues.

Shekhar: Yes, you are right. But from its length, it is like a men's hair too.

Manoj: Okay. Now, let us find out whose hair it is.

Manoj hung and started investigating on it and ask his team to bring all the guestlist who were present in Mr.

Bose's party. It was a personal party so there were no CCTV cameras or photo shoots allowed. His team bifurcated the names of those who were close to Mr. Bose. Meantime, Manoj started questioning Mr. Khanna.

Manoj: You said you were friends with Mr. Bose. What do you know about him?

Mr. Khanna: We are only professional friends. All I know about his business and work. I don't know anything more than that.

Manoj: Mr. Khanna, you know I am a calm person and when I lose it, you know what I can do. I wanted to do this very calmly. But okay, let us choose the other way. Manoj came outside of the room and brought a plastic bag and a file. Mr. Khanna feared after seeing this.

Mr. Khanna: What is this? You are not allowed to hit me. You can't torture a person like that. You don't know who I am and what my power is. I want to talk to my lawyer.

Manoj: I can, and I will. I have evidence that you are supplying illegal drugs in your hotels, parties, and bars. Also, you have a pharmaceutical factory which supplies fake medicines, right? I have so much evidence of you. This is an FIR against you. You want to tell the truth or see the jail? The choice is totally yours Mr. Khanna.

Mr. Khanna: What? Who complaint against me? This is all fake.

Manoj: Yes, it is a fake FIR. But I can make it real. These are two option Infront of you. One, you answer only those questions that I ask and two, I forget about Mr. Bose's case and starts a new case against you.

Because of you, I will get appreciation from the department, high salary, and more power.

Mr. Khanna was too scared. He was getting worried and started sweating.

Manoj: You are here, bag is here, file is here so, choose wisely. I will surely be going to hurt you so bad, but there will be no scratch, no blood, nothing left on your body. You can complain to me when you find any evidence.

Mr. Khanna: Okay, okay. I will answer. Ask me whatever you want to know. But please don't hurt me or case a file. I will close all my illegal businesses.

Manoj: Well, I am happy to hear that you are helping a police to solve the case. So, tell me everything you know about Mr. Bose and his Black illegal businesses.

Mr. Khanna: We all know his good side, but bad side was, he had an illegal club, bars in various places in India. That pharmaceutical company was started by him but, he does not want to ruin his positive image so, he gave it to me. On all the legal papers will have my name, but those are all fake. He was one of the partners in that with 20% of the share, and mine was 10%. Also, he was supplying drugs from different states to India. He has contacts for intoxicants. Not only cocaine, but he also supplied weed, LSD, alcohol, and all types of toxicants.

Manoj: Rest of the shares? Is there anyone who is involved in this business.

Mr. Khanna: There are lots of small % shareholders, who didn't even know what an owner can do. They were only investing and in return, they received profit.

Mr. Khanna: No. I told you everything I knew. He has so many friends who handled those businesses. I don't know their names or any details.

Manoj: We found a hair at crime scene. It did not match either Kavya or Mr. Bose. It means it is a person's hair who killed Mr. Bose and saved your daughter. You knew him very well. So, is there anyone who is jealous of Mr. Bose's?

Mr. Khanna: I told you earlier. I know nothing about it. If someone killed him for money, then why from Top fifty? Why not from Top Twenty-Five businessman? There is someone who protected Mr. Bose till the end, who protected me and there are some more like me. I don't know who he is, what is his name or anything. But whenever we were in any trouble, he was the one who helped us.

Manoj: You know what he did to your daughter, and still, you are protecting that person? Why? Who is he?

Mr. Khanna: It is my personal reason. I will tell the names of all the places where he has illegal business and drugs. But could not tell that name. If I do, then he can finish each of my close ones.

Manoj: You are the worst parent I have even seen. Mr. Bose was trying to rape your daughter. He had done similarly with so many girls out there. Hopefully, they filed a complaint against him, but due to money and that person you are talking about, Mr. Bose always survived. What would happen if Mr. Bose were alive and you found this. What will you do?

Mr. Khanna: Neither Kavya is my daughter nor Mrs. Khanna is my wife. I never married to that woman. I am not married to anyone. It was a mistake for which I am paying.

Manoj: What? What do you just say?

Mr. Khanna: I... I am sorry for whatever I said. The sentence was not part of the investigation. As I said, it is a personal matter. Make a deal, I will give you all the information and you will never try to meet me again. Is it okay?

Manoj: Actually, we don't deal here like this. You must come here whenever I call. You can't run from this city anymore. Santosh, take all the details from him and rest action we will do later.

Mr. Khanna stands from his chair without saying anything. After giving all details about Mr. Bose businesses and friends who helped him, he was about to leave police station. Mrs. Khanna and Kavya were with Anaya at his lab for examination.

Mr. Khanna: I am not running. He will not even let me run away. In fact, he will not even let me live after this. And don't try to ask anything about me or my business to Mrs. Khanna. She knows nothing.

Manoj: What? Wait.

Manoj was curious. He tried to stop him, but he walked fast into his car and left. Suddenly, he realizes something.

Manoj: Santosh! Where is Mr. Khanna? Where is he?

Santosh: He left sir. What happened?

Manoj: He was talking about someone else who can destroy him, and many more. Ask the team to catch him. Go, go. Follow him and get him back.

Santosh left with the driver and started to follow him.

Manoj: He mentioned about someone, but… My mind only heard about Mr. Bose's name and story. He said all the things, but… I want to hear Mr. Bose from his name, and he is the culprit. It is my fault.

Mr. Khanna left, and Santosh did not know where he was going. Santosh tries to follow him. Mr. Khanna finally reached his home path. Santosh followed him and he was about to reach his house. After a few minutes, a gunshot sound came. Santosh entered the house curiously and went upstairs. He saw Mr. Khanna shoot himself in the head. Santosh called Manoj to inform him of this incidence.

Santosh: Sir, Mr. Khanna is dead. He shot himself on his head.

Manoj: What? Where? How? Call an ambulance and I am sending force. We are coming. Don't let anyone enter the house.

**

Manoj set out at crime scene with his team. He called Anaya to inform his wife and daughter about the scene.

Manoj: Anaya, Is Mrs. Khanna and Kavya still with you?

Anaya: Yes. What happened?

Manoj: Mr. Kha… Mr. Khanna shot himself.

Anaya: Oh god. How? Where?

Manoj: Not much but, he was afraid of someone. He said, 'He won't let me run or live'. Don't know what he was talking about.

Anaya: You can interrogate to Mrs. Khanna. Maybe She knows something, and she can help.

Manoj: Before suicide, he told me not to ask anything about his wife as she knows nothing. I could not believe him if he would not die though. Just take your team, Mrs. Khanna, to their house immediately.

Manoj hung up the call. Anaya does not have any idea how she tells his daughter this situation. Anaya slowly went to Mrs. Khanna and stood beside her. Mrs. Khanna was in deep thinking. Anaya touched her shoulder and Mrs. Khanna stunned. She looked at Anaya and stood up curiously.

Mrs. Khanna: What? What happened to my daughter?

Anaya: Mrs. Khanna, we have to leave at your house.

Mrs. Khanna: My house? Why? What happened?

Anaya: I am sorry to say this to you but, Mr. Khanna committed suicide. He shot himself.

Mrs. Khanna could not stand and started crying. Anaya tried to control the situation and take her to their house.

Anaya called Shekhar and informed her about it.

Shekhar: We are examining Kavya. How can I tell her that his father is dead?

Anaya: I know. I know that it is too hard to say a sixteen-year-old girl, and harder to handle her in this situation. A girl is always a Princess for his father, and a father always a King for her. Do one thing, don't tell her anything now. Shekhar, Get the team and come to the crime scene.

**

Anaya, Shekhar and Mrs. Khanna reached Mr. Khanna's home. They went to the room. Mrs. Khanna started crying after seeing Mr. Khanna's body covered by white cloth. There was a crime scene tape. Anaya and Shekhar started looking everywhere for a clue, but she found nothing.

Manoj: It is a suicide, but something or someone else forced him to do this.

Anaya: Yes, it is definitely a suicide case.

Shekhar: What to do now?

Manoj: There is some mastermind behind this who is making all of them dancing on his hand. We need to figure out who he is. Santosh, give me all the details about who is available at that party. But first, all the illegal businesses of Mr. Khanna will have to be closed. From that, we will find the secret of that third person.

Anaya looked at Mrs. Khanna who was crying lying on Mr. Khanna's dead body. Anaya looked at Manoj and he was standing stir looking at her. His eyes were wet. Manoj constantly looked at her. After a few seconds, Manoj took his goggles and put them on. Anaya went at Mrs. Khanna and held her shoulder.

Anaya: Mrs. Khanna, please control yourself. I know it is hard to believe that your closest one is no more. You have to take care of your daughter too. Kavya is just a teenager; she could not handle the stress. I know how it feels when father was away and there are only two women at home. They have to take care of the house, themselves, and fight with society. For a girl, we thought whatever will happen in our life, my father will take care of me. I hope you both will take care of yourself.

Anaya looked at Shekhar and Shekhar sent his body to postmortem as Mr. Khanna asked to donate his most of the organs to needy people. Mrs. Khanna was leaving from there and stopped at Manoj.

Mrs. Khanna: Can you please tell me his last words? Manoj, you took him to investigation room. What happened there? What he confesses? Why had he shot himself?

Manoj replied without looking at her and removing goggles. He was not able to make eye contact with a person who recently lost his loved one. Manoj feels that he could save Mr. Khanna if he listened his statement clearly rather than listening only about Mr. Bose.

Manoj: I know you will have so many questions. Society will ask you questions, and you could not answer those. I only want to say to you that, Mr. Khanna confesses his illegal businesses in India, and we will close them soon.

Mrs. Khanna: Okay. I will not ask you anything about it. But what will I answer my daughter? What will I tell him when she asks me about his father?

Manoj stood stir without saying or moving. Anaya looked at him and replied to Mrs. Khanna.

Anaya: Just tell her that, his father was a great guy. He was a hero who saved millions of lives by giving his statement and killing himself. People and media will raise so many questions to you all the time. I suggest you move to the other country where you can start a new journey. Where people ask less questions than here. Where Kavya can continue his study and lighten up her future. Whatever Mr. Khanna did in his life, but he has to remember that, if you ever take any decision about yourself, then think about what will happen to your closest ones.

**

In a few months, Mrs. Khanna, and Kavya both left to other country to start their new life. Sometimes, when something ends, it starts new things.

**

After a few days, blood results came from the dead bodies of suppliers and Mr. Bose. The drug was anabolic-androgenic steroids. It was man-made version of testosterone. Healthcare provides to treat some hormone problems in men, delayed in puberty, and muscle loss from some diseases. But some people get addicted and misuse it.

Anaya: It is not good. People are using it like a… it is addictive. It is used for medication and not for addiction. If situation remains the same, then there will be more rape and more murders in city. It should be stopped.

Shekhar: It will be. Someday.

*****

**

People who have Money can do anything right or wrong and still will never be get caught. And if they caught, Money would shut the door of laws. God will punish them in hell, and they will live on earth like heaven. But life for victim and their family being like hell.

Lady justice have a blind fold and a weigh balance in one hand. People who have Money and Power thinks that the Lady Justice will only judge from wight balance in one hand. But forgot the Sword. Lady Justice cannot fight in this cruel world now, but some other Lady can take Justice either way.

In today's world, if you have either money or power, you can control anything. But forgot that, if you have courage, you can face everything.

New Delhi. 21st August 2015

Manoj and his team still struggling to find mastermind who forced Mr. Khanna to kill himself, and murderer of Mr. Bose's case. Manoj submitted the file of Mr. Khanna's confessions of Mr. Bose's to the court and all illegal businesses have been closed. Mr. Khanna families shifted to London and Mr. Bose families shifted to Switzerland. Society still asks questions and make allegations on their death. But they must move on from the past to start the present and make a new future.

**

Santosh enters in Manoj's cabin. He sees Manoj is in stress, thinking about something.
Santosh: What happened sir?
Manoj: It has been more than four months and still the Mr. Bose's case could not close.
Santosh: Case was closed, sir. Mr. Bose is dead, Mr. Bose and Mr. Khanna's illegal business shut down, and both families started a new life happily. What opens now?
Manoj: I did not hear what Mr. Khanna said. Someone was protecting Mr. Bose. Someone involved in this game long back. Someone who is the mastermind of all of this. We could not find a hint that gave us courage. Mr. Bose had done a terrible thing, but that murderer was not supposed to punish him. For that, there is a law. We have a hair sample but what to do with it. I must catch him in any situation.

Santosh: Sir, do you think he is a villain? But I think he is a hero. He is a savior. Not only I, but so many people out there were thinking he was a hero, who saved Kavya's life. He had done that thing that police could not do. Kavya can live happily right now. But there are so many girls living in this world who can't even file a complaint because of society. So many people say, 'don't file a complaint. If her name comes in media, then no one will marry such a girl.'

Manoj: You know right that we have a justice society named Court. We can file a case with proper evidence and criminal will sentence to death if he or she found guilty.

Santosh: There are so many cases pending in court. Don't know when it will close. We had all the evidence against Mr. Bose rape and illegal businesses, and we closed that file. You should feel happy that it is close. That day during interrogation, you asked Mr. Khanna 'What if Mr. Bose alive and rape your daughter?' You know the outcomes, that is why you said it.

Manoj: Why should I happy? We can submit all the evidence to court, Mr. Bose is found guilty, and the court will give him punishment. It should go like this and not murder him and then close his business.

Santosh: Sir, I don't want to fight against you on this topic. But there are so many rape cases are still pending. Better to close that and then decide who is right or wrong.

Santosh left after saying this and Manoj kept thinking about his words.

Chapter 2
Your enemy is way closer than your friends & family.

4.24 - A Date & A Time

New Delhi. 11th December 2015

It was Ten O'clock in the morning. Manoj was sitting in his chair working on Mr. Bose's cases. Suddenly his mobile rungs. It was Police commissioner Akhilesh Shrivastava.

Akhilesh: Manoj, this is Akhilesh speaking.

Manoj: Good morning, sir.

Commissioner: Good morning. Hope you remembered Mr. Bose's case. We have got a new case similar as well connected to Mr. Bose's case. A girl named Akanksha Patil found brutally raped and dead in Noida's Sector 1 with one more dead. Rapist was murdered after the rape. I want you to catch that murderer who is murdering the rapist. We have a law for that, court for that. If all people murder all the time, then we don't require court and judge in this country. This is second rape case in Nine months, and I would like to manage this case to you and that forensic girl who helped you in Mr. Bose's case. I hope you both will find evidence and catch whoever is behind it. I have a meeting with PM related to rise on rape cases in our state. Manoj, I hope that you will not disappoint me.

Manoj: Okay sir. I will investigate it and my team will catch him soon sir. I will not disappoint you. Jai hind sir.

Commissioners hang up the call.

Manoj: Santosh, we got a new case. I got a call from the Commissioner. Last time you said that the that person whoever is killing rapist is a savior, right? He can save girls or women without killing rapist till he found guilty in court. He will surely be punished for what he has done. I could not meet him last time, but now even God wants me to catch him and punish him for his action. Come on, let us go for a drive.

In a few minutes Manoj receives a call from Anaya.

Anaya: I got a call from Commissioner. He didn't inform about the case. We are on our way to the crime scene. Anything about victims?

Manoj: We are leaving from here too. We will reach each other in a few minutes. I will ask my team to get all the details of the accused and murderer. We will discuss it there.

Manoj hugs up the call.

**

Manoj reached at given destination. It is a mansion, and it belongs to Mr. Jain. Manoj was shocked seeing him in his own bloody river.

***

Mr. Jain was a Politician and mafia. Also, everybody knows that he supplies LSD & Cocaine to VIPs at rave parties, hotels & bars. But nobody can catch him because he has a direct connection with the CM of state. Mr. Bose, Mr. Khanna, Mr. Sisodia and Mr. Luthra asked him to provide drugs whenever their guest requested.

***

Manoj: It is Mr. Jain's case. He is a criminal then why did the commissioner call and ask him to manage the case? He is a devil by the way. If he is dead, then we must celebrate his death anniversary. But he was a politician, so we must declare him a martyr even if we don't want to. Santosh, have you got anything about that girl?

Santosh was a bit curious and felt stress while answering that. He seats a lot. He took a handkerchief and cleaned sweatshirt.

Manoj: What happened Santosh? Why are you so stressed just giving the information? Who was Akanksha Patil?

Santosh: Sir, Akanksha Patil was a daughter in law of CM Yogita Patil. Yesterday was her birthday and turned seventeen. Mr. Jain mixed something in her drink and took at this Mansion and rape. This is a profoundly serious case.

Manoj: Oh, God. That is why Commissioner Akhilesh directly contacted the case. CM was feeding the snake, Santosh. Grab the details of that party. Every guest list and even the servants who were present. Let's see what will happen.

Manoj enters the Mansion and finds there are two bodies available. One is Mr. Jain, and the second one is Mr. Sisodia.

***

Mr. Sisodia was a competitor of Mr. Bose. They were each other's enemies. Mr. Sisodia was always down in business from Mr. Bose. After the death of Mr. Bose, he was the happiest person on earth. Although, Mr. Sisodia was the younger brother of Mr. Jain.

***

Manoj: It is not only about Mr. Jain. It is about Mr. Sisodia too. What will happened yesterday? Santosh, go and check everything. Try to find CCTV or a witness if any.

**

Anaya and Shekhar arrived at the gate. Anaya parked her car, and both walked inside the mansion.

Shekhar: What do you think? Who will be in there?

Anaya: Don't you think if I know about it, I will inform you? The Commissioner didn't inform anything of this case.

Shekhar: Yes… yes. You are right. But you know what I think?

Anaya: What?

Shekhar: I think that there will be a businessman or a mafia who was trying to rape a girl. But that girl defend herself and killed them.

Anaya: What if they were having drug dealing and someone attacked or deceive, and people got killed?

Shekhar: Nah. If there was a drug dealing, then Commissioner won't be involved. I think… Last night, two people were trying to rape a girl. That girl tried to run from them, but they caught her. They tried to remove her clothes in lust. To resist and defense, she slapped or hurt one of them. He got angry, and then he slapped that girl so hard that she gained consciousness.

Anaya was afraid of listening to this. She started sweating.

Shekhar: Then they started rape to her, but that man not satisfied with it. Then, that man insert a rod to satisfy his ego.

Anaya: Stop. What? What? Why? I mean why… Stop. Let's go and check the situation.

Shekhar got scared and walked behind Anaya.

**

They got stunned after looking at this. She was clueless about saying anything.

Anaya: What happened here? Is this Mr. Jain and Mr. Sisodia? Are they both victims?

Manoj: No. These are the culprits or rapists I say. The victim is a girl named Akanksha Patil.

Anaya and Shekhar both looked at each other.

Manoj: She should be upstairs.

Anaya and Shekhar ran upstairs. When they reached there, the body was covered with white cloth. Due to excessive blood loss, white cloth becomes red from some parts. Anaya removed a slight cloth and sees her mouth bitten very badly. She slowly removed more and sees her chest, neck and back had so many fingernail scratches. Anaya looked down at her and saw that two metal rods were still inserted in her private parts. Anaya is shocked to see all this. She could not stand there and ran towards the gallery to vomit. Shekhar saw this and ran behind to help her. Shekhar gave her water.

Anaya: What is this? How cruel are they? Which animal can do such kind of act? Their lust increased so much that they had done this.

Shekhar: Humans ma'am. Animals don't do that, but humans do. How does the person's lust increase so much that he rapes someone. If he does not get that much satisfaction they want, then puts a hand, bottle and now a rod inside them. Seeing such people, I wish

I were a dog, cat, or a mouse. People like these have questioned being human.

Santosh and Anaya stand stir for a while.

Anaya: Nirbhaya rape case. It took 8 years to solve. Suryanelli rape case took 4 years to solve. Shakti mills rape case took 1 year to solve. Priyanka Reddy rape case took a month. Now, Kavya and Akanksha rape case which solved in a day. Whoever killing such rapist, doing good job. At least these girls' parents will not eat the shocks of the court and police station to find their daughter's rapist. Let's start our work.

Anaya and Shekhar started their investigation after taking a deep breath. They found various drugs, bloods which is related to three of them only. They got three whiskey bottles and glasses. During the investigation, Shekhar finds a little part of a black-colored cloth with skin on Mr. Sisodia's nail.

Anaya: It should be a clue to that Person who killed them.

Shekhar: Ma'am, we found four people's footprints. In Mr. Bose's case we did not get any footprint. We are so close to catching him.

Anaya: Great. Let's see how many are there. There are four different footprints available. Three must be the dead ones and the other will be the savior. Santosh, please check if it matches with all three or not.

Shekhar tried to match the footprints with Mr. Jain, Mr. Sisodia and Akanksha.

Shekhar: Ma'am, three footprints matched and only one is different. Shoe size must be seven numbers and

if we see the angles, it is formal shoes. Last time Kavya said that whoever saved him wore black formal shoes.
Anaya: Okay. Shekhar sent the body for examination. We will see those footprints.

**

Manoj and his team were trying to find any suspects or clue near Mansion.
Manoj: Santosh, have you got any?
Santosh: No sir. I asked security guard, but yesterday nearly Two O'clock at midnight, Mr. Jain arrived here with Mr. Sisodia. Mr. Sisodia gave him Two Thousand Rupees and asked him to leave.
Manoj: What? This country is not progressing because of this corruption. Call him right now.
Santosh calls the security guard.
Manoj: What's your name?
Security Guard: Rakesh, sir. Sir, please let me go, sir. I don't know anything. Jain sir comes many times with Sisodia sir. He always gave me Two Thousand Rupees and asked me to leave. I have no idea what is happening there. They always told me to come next day by Ten O'clock for cleaning. I always found a bottle, plastic bags with powder only. I know nothing else. When I arrived this morning, I saw that Mr. Jain and Mr. Sisodia both were dead. I was shocked and I called the police. I don't know more than this sir. Please sir.
Manoj: Okay, okay. Go. Santosh, I asked you to get those party's details. Have you got any?
Santosh: Our team is working on it. We will get it in a few hours.

4.24 - A Date & A Time

Manoj: Tell them to work fast. We will receive a call for an update at any minute now.

**

Manoj and Santosh went at Akanksha. At first, they both were horrified seeing that. Santosh could not stand there and left. Manoj felt angry and sad at the same time. His eyes were red and had tears in them.

Manoj: What have you got?

Anaya: We got lots of clues today. This time hopefully we will find that person who killed all these rapists. Can you please get details of last night's party?

Manoj: I already told my team to work on it. Why do you need that?

Anaya: I need some blood or hair samples of his friends, family, and enemies especially.

Manoj: We are gathering their details and sending you those details and samples as soon as we receive them.

Anaya: Till then, we will examine the bodies in our lab. If we find anything, then we will let you know. Shekhar, please arrange to send the bodies to the lab.

**

After two hours of research on Akanksha's party details, Manoj gets a call from Santosh.

Manoj: Yes, Santosh. What happened?

Santosh: We list down all the relatives who were present at the party. And we got names of the enemies of Mr. Jain and Mr. Sisodia too.

Manoj: Great. We will meet at the police station.

After hanging up the call, Manoj got a call from CM. She was sad and overwhelmed.

CM: Inspector Manoj. This is Yogita Patil.

Manoj: Jai hind ma'am.

CM: Jai hind. I need the status of your job. What you and your team is doing?

Manoj: We got lots of clues today related to that person who killed Mr. Jain and Mr. Sisodia. We made a strategy to catch that murderer.

CM: Where is my granddaughter now? What about Mr. Jain & Mr. Sisodia? Where are they?

Manoj: We transferred all the three dead bodies in cold storage. Ma'am, from this scenario we might thinking that they both kidnapped your granddaughter yesterday and…

CM sobbed a little and started crying.

CM: Manoj, remember that whenever you say something, there should be a justification behind it. Hope you have something before you said this line.

Manoj: We have ma'am. The team is examining the bodies; they will provide a report of whatever I said.

CM: Hmm. After your team examines both dead bodies, let me know. I want to do something with them.

CM hung up the call. Dead bodies sent at the lab for postmortem.

**

Anaya and Shekhar leave the lab. They both in car and Shekhar sees scratch marks on Anaya's hand.

Shekhar: Ma'am! What happened to your hand?

Anaya: Stop calling me Ma'am Shekhar. We both are the same age, and you were my classmates once.

Shekhar: It was a different time. At that time, we both had the same position, but now you are my senior. By the way what happened to your hand?

Anaya: It is nothing. I have a cat and recently she gets little aggressive because we took her to doctor. She has not eaten for the last few days and is puking all the time. She got angry so she scratched and bit me.

Shekhar: Oh, wild cat.

They are talking and Anaya receives a call from her mother.

Ammi: Assalamualikum, Anaya. Where are you?

Anaya: At work Ammi. We are going to the lab right now. What happened?

Ammi: Nothing. Just curious if you are okay or not. Have you eaten something? Have you taken your medicines?

Anaya: I have eaten well, and I will take medicine later. I have lots of work to do. Khuda hafiz.

Ammi: Okay, okay. But remember...

Anaya: Yes, Ammi. I am not responsible for anything happening around. Now, please don't worry, I will take care of myself.

Anaya hung up the call.

Shekhar: What happened to you? What medicines are you taking?

Anaya: Nothing. I have a Sugar problem.

Shekhar: Okay. I know it is your personal thing, but I heard it so many times that is why I could not control to ask this. Why is your mother always telling you that 'You are not responsible for anything.'?

Ammi: I don't know. It has been so many years and in all cases that victim or rapists' death by rape, she always says that.
Shekhar: Did you not ask your mother about it?
Anaya: I asked too many times, but she always says that 'You will find it when time comes.' And after all these years, I am just waiting to find out why Ammi says that. Neither did I ask her again nor did she answer.
Shekhar: Did you not ask your father about it?
Anaya became a little sad after hearing this. She froze for some time. She starts remembering childhood memories she used to spend with her family. Two little girls are running in an empty garden. Laughing, playing with mother and father. Suddenly, the phone rang. Anaya picked and it is Manoj.
Manoj: We have got some blood, skin, and hair samples as required. Sending to your lab for examination. Call me if you get any clue.
Anaya hung up without saying anything.

**

Anaya and Shekhar reached the lab and walked inside.
Shekhar: What happened?
Anaya: It is Manoj. They got some samples to check.
Shekhar: Okay. But our talk was incomplete. Weren't you asked your father?
Anaya: We will continue this investigation later. First, start with dead bodies.
Shekhar and Anaya start to examine both dead bodies. They took blood samples first. She asked Shekhar to get Mr. Bose's report to match.

Anaya: Mr. Bose's blood was dry, that is why we could not get any clues about which drug he took. But, after this incident they took the same drug. It was anabolic-androgenic steroids which gives more strength. It is prohibited in India but, we know no one can stop Mr. Jain to import from outside.

Shekhar: Mr. Sisodia's lever is damaged because of Alcohol consumption. Let me see marks on bodies.

Shekhar removes cloths from both bodies. They have similar marks on belly and when he naked the body, they find private parts cut in half.

Anaya: Whoever killed them was the same as before. There are so many scars and skin ripped with nails. It is because Akanksha was pushing them maybe and they both enjoyed it because of lust. Shekhar, check whether they have some other person's fingerprints or not. And we got a skin from Mr. Sisodia's nail, right? Try to match it with samples we receive.

Shekhar started the match with all samples that receives from Manoj. But no sample matches it. But Anaya found different fingering on Mr. Jain's body. Anaya called Manoj to inform it.

Anaya: Hello Manoj, we examine and find that Mr. Sisodia and Mr. Jain both took anabolic-androgenic steroid before rape. None of the sample you sent were matched with received Mr. Sisodia's nail. Also, their body's private part is cut in half same as Mr. Bose. Conclusion is that the person who killed three of them are the same. Luckily, we found a different fingerprint on Mr. Jain's body. If the skin samples were not matched with your ones, then definitely the fingerprints will be someone else's.

Manoj: Thanks for the information. I had guessed that no sample would match. Anyway, if I get any clue, I'll call you.

Manoj hung up and Anaya starts research again.

Shekhar: Ma'am, can we start research on Akanksha?

**

The doors opened, and security guards entered the room. Shekhar and Anaya were shocked.

Shekhar: Hey! What are you doing? Who are you?

Anaya: You are not allowed to enter without permission. Who are you?

CM enters in the room from behind security guards. Her eyes were red, and she looked angry. Anaya and Shekhar shocked and stood stirred for a while.

CM: I'm sorry Ms. Anaya Kadri to come like this. But I don't need anyone's permission to enter anywhere.

Anaya: I'm sorry ma'am. I don't know if it is you.

CM: Where is my granddaughter?

Shekhar: She is in cold storage, ma'am. We are about to postmortem and examine her.

CM: I want to see her first.

Anaya, Shekhar, and CM goes to cold storage. Shekhar is a little worried while opening the door.

CM: What? Open the door.

Anaya: Ma'am, please control your emotions after seeing this.

Shekhar opened the door. Because her face was bitten very badly, CM got a little scared seeing this.

Anaya: Ma'am, are you okay?

CM: Remove the cloth.
Anaya: Ma'am...
CM: I said, remove it.
Shekhar removes the cloth. Seeing her granddaughter in this condition, she was scared, breaths heavily and could not hold her tears. She was stunned and stood stir for a while. After a few seconds, she leaves the cold storage. Anaya and her bodyguard ran behind her.
Anaya: Ma'am, are you okay?
CM: No. I am not okay.
CM sobbed and started crying. Anaya tried to calm her down.
Anaya: Please ma'am. Control yourself.
CM: When I become CM, I thought I have power, support, money and no one can even touch me. But they scoundrel.
She cried continuously.
CM: My son died in a car accident. Akanksha's mother was permanent when he died. Later, her mother died as soon as she born to Akanksha. I was so alone and felt depressed. I only had Akanksha in my life. I gave her all the love that she never had. The love of mother and father. We always celebrated her birthday happily but last night. She was only seventeen years old. Manoj said that Mr. Jain and Mr. Sisodia kidnapped her and raped her. Do you have any evidence that they done this? Let's go to the lab.
Anaya brought all the evidence she found.
Anaya: Ma'am, we matched the fingerprints, skin, and blood from Akanksha's body to Mr. Jain and Mr.

Sisodia's samples. It matched perfectly. We are about to match the sperm that found from her too.

CM: Test it now and tell me.

Anaya started examination and, in few minutes, results came.

Anaya: Ma'am, both samples matched perfectly. They both raped her brutally and…

CM: Okay.

Anaya: We have also got skin and ripped cloth of a murderer in Mr. Sisodia's nail.

CM: I am not interested in murderer. And he is not a murderer, he is a savior. He provided justice. If they both were alive, I could not find who raped and killed my granddaughter. At least, her culprits got punished in this life.

CM's personal assistant came and inform that Manoj asks for interrogation. She nodded her head.

CM: Anaya. Once you complete the examinations of both bodies, inform me. I want to process these two rapists. People out there who thinks to rape will remember not to do such kind of things.

CM leaves the lab to go to the Police station.

**

CM arrives at Manoj's police station at Two O'clock. All the policemen stood up and salute her. She and personal assistant enters in Manoj's cabin and CM sits in front of him. Manoj stood and shocked while seeing this.

Manoj: Ma'am, what happened? Why did you come here?

CM: You asked me for interrogation. Ask me whatever you want to ask.

Manoj: Ma'am, I would have come to your office if…

CM: If I want you to work then you must come to my office, and if you want me to work then I can too. Please sit and do your work. Right now, I am just a person who came here for interrogation, treat me that way.

Manoj: Okay ma'am. Santosh, grab three cups of tea for us.

CM: You provide this service to all suspects, or I am CM that's why?

Manoj: This is how I work ma'am. I always give tea or coffee to whoever enters this gate of the police station.

CM: I like your working style, Manoj. Now, let's start.

Manoj: How do you know Mr. Jain and Mr. Sisodia?

CM: Before entering politics, I was a social worker. They both were working with me. Jain was a punk since childhood. If someone is to be intimidated, threatened, or bullied, we asked him to do it. Sisodia was like me. Smart, sincere, good at management. He wants to be the world's richest person. I was friends with Sisodia. We both met once while we were socially working, and Jain his older brother. With time, our bond became very strong. We were like three musketeers. We solve problems so fast, which government took time. Seeing our growing name and work, one day CM of state asked me and Sisodia to join their party and stands for post of MLA in election. We three sat that night and decide that I will stand for the MLA, Sisodia will be the richest businessman and Jain will do same work that he used to do. I accepted to become MLA in 1998. Later, I helped Sisodia to open Hotels, Bars, Clubs with power and gave him money that he wanted. If someone rejects our proposal, then we ask Jain to complete the offer. We know each other from 1991. It's been more than 20 years since I know them. But after this incident, I don't know them.

Manoj: Okay. You said you helped them to grow business, market, and all. Do you know that they are supplying illegal drugs to their VIPs? They import drugs from foreign to India. They were polluting the city.

CM kept silent without saying anything.

Manoj: Ma'am, they took anabolic-androgenic steroids before doing the thing with your granddaughter. You must tell the truth. We need evidence so we can close businesses like Mr. Bose's.

CM: Yes. They did not inform me but when I found out I scolded them.

Manoj: You knew. You scolded them, and then what? They cried, right? But you did not close those businesses? You stand with them? There are so many respected Police Inspectors who had FIR against them, but because of supremacy, rule, and assurance that CM will always help them, they survived.

CM: I did not stand with them Manoj. I know they were doing wrong but… I don't want to share it with you. It was a personal matter.

Manoj: Sorry ma'am but right now nothing is personal. I know you do want to close that business too, but it would affect your friendship, business, and chair of CM.

CM looked him with Anger. She wanted to say something in her defense, deep down she knows that Manoj was saying the truth.

Manoj: It is still not too late. We have evidence, victims, and files ready to submit to the court. Your role in this will be the highest and it will affect your CM position too.

CM did not say anything.

Manoj: Anyways, can you please let us know about that party? Your granddaughter's birthday party. What happened there?

CM: Akanksha turned seventeen that day. Her parents weren't alive, that is why I threw a party for her. It was organized in our mansion. Jain was handling all decorations, preparation and invitations to his friends and mine. It was Twelve O'clock, and we cut the cake. There were mostly kids available, and all were her friends. Everyone was happy, dancing and playing games. Sisodia was not present at that moment. I asked Jain to call him. Around 1:30 PM Sisodia came. Jain and Sisodia were enjoying the party, playing with kids and after few minutes they both went outside. I doubted they went to consume alcohol or drugs. Eventually, Jain did not even touch any drug from the past seven months. Once Jian was highly addictive to drugs because he supplies. But we helped him to pull from that mud. He was in rehab for more than two years before continuing. Later, I got a call from high command so came outside to talk. The call was about twenty minutes. When I came to the party, I saw kids were playing but Akanksha was not there. We asked her friends, parents, servants and searched everywhere but could not find her.

Manoj: Haven't you asked Mr. Jain & Mr. Sisodia?

CM: I called them Jain. When Jain was in rehab, Sisodia started consuming Alcohol and slowly it became his habit. Sisodia consume Alcohol like water. Jain said Sisodia's having problem with lever, so he took him to doctor in city.

Manoj: They said, and you believed them?

Santosh came into the cabin.

Santosh: Sir, I am sorry. But all shops are closed so could not bring tea for CM ma'am.

Manoj nodded his head.

CM: Do you believe him?

Manoj: Pardon?

CM: How long have you been working with him?

Manoj: Nearly One year. But why?

CM: CM is sitting in front of you, you asked him to bring tea, he took Twenty-Five minutes to search and replied that all shops are closed. Do you not want to go outside and check whether shops are open or not?

Manoj: I trust him. Why would I do…

CM: Exactly. I believed him because I had known them for many years, their situations. I don't know what happened there and who killed Jain and Sisodia, but I need their bodies after examinations on them. I want to do something that people out there will never even think to rape.

4.24 - A Date & A Time

CM stood up and walked towards the door. Manoj shouted from behind.

Manoj: It can harm your reputation. Everyone knows who gave the approval of those businesses, and what was your relationship with those people.

CM: I know Manoj what I am doing. Akanksha's culprits got their punishment, but the one who encouraged them was me. I knew all of this but still I kept quiet. I knew they were drug addicts, If I had stopped them earlier, then today my granddaughter would be alive. By morning, you will get all those details. You can do whatever you want to do Manoj. And yes, if someone interferes in this work then tell me.

Manoj: Is there anyone else in this?

CM: What you are doing will bring him out of his cave.

CM leaves after that. Manoj understood that there is someone who handled CM position too. CM Yogita Patil was not the one who handled this. Manoj got curious to find that mastermind.

Manoj: There is someone else in this Mistry which is connected to Mr. Bose and Mr. Khanna's business and death. Santosh, do one thing. Search everything in a radius of 10 km of CM's mansion. We will surely get something from there.

Santosh: 10 km? Manoj sir, city border comes in less than 6 km radius. I don't think they will go to the city and come again to Mr. Jain's mansion. And Mr. Jain and Mr. CM's Mansion was not that close sir. It will be almost 6 k from there.

Manoj: Maybe you are right. But the way CM has told, my suspicion should be correct. If Mr. Sisodia is highly addicted to alcohol, he surely went to a shop to purchase.

Santosh: How come you be so sure?

Manoj: I know that there is a tea stall in the side street. Why didn't you bring tea from there?

Santosh: She is CM. It doesn't feel good if we give them tea from a small tea stall.

Manoj: Exactly. I know there is a tea stall, but you said all Shops are closed. Eventually you are not wrong too. Same as, they said they took him to city. They also went to the doctor, but later they bought alcohol. Neither CM asked about it nor did they say. Go and get the details.

Santosh left with team from the police station.

**

Santosh came after a few hours.

Santosh: Sir, we got CCTV footage of Mr. Jain's car near the clinic. They were truly in the city. They went to the clinic at midnight around 1:45. After fifteen minutes, they left and at 2:05 PM, they stopped at a wine shop, but they did not buy anything.

Manoj: What? We found a bottle at mansion. What have they bought from there? Santosh let's check what they sell. Also, we will check the clinic too. What is his name?

Santosh: Dr. Somai.

Manoj nodded his head. Manoj and Santosh leave for the clinic.

**

4.24 - A Date & A Time

Manoj and Santosh arrived at clinic. It was a very small clinic. He does not have patient after all.

Manoj: This looks strange. He has nothing here. My bathroom is as much as its clinic. Look at the board, it says B.A.M.S. Why did they come here? Something is very wrong.

Santosh: Is he selling that drug?

They both entered and sat in front of Dr. Somai.

Dr. Somai: Hello Inspector. How can I help you?

Manoj: I am addicted to something and want that thing. I heard from someone that only you are supplying.

Dr. Somai was afraid. He felt sweaty. He hesitated to talk further.

Dr. Somai: Wh... What? What are you asking, Inspector? What addiction? I give medicine to the patients nor drugs.

Manoj: Medicine is also a drug doctor. Please give it sir. I can't tell you the name of the person who gave me your address otherwise I will. I only want one tablet, nothing else.

Dr. Somai: Look Inspector, you are making false allegations against me. I have no clue what you are talking about.

Manoj: Dr. Somai, I am not making false allegations on you. Okay. Mr. Jain and Mr. Sisodia are my friends and they both told me about anabolic-androgenic steroids. You gave it to him and not me? We are friends.

Dr. Somai: I... I don't know anyone of them. Please Inspector, leave.

Manoj: Okay, then.

Manoj stood up and closed the door. He took out his pistol.

Dr. Somai: What… What are you doing? Why did you close the door? I did not do anything. He…

Before Dr. Somai shouted for help, Santosh held his mouth and silenced him. He made him sit on the chair.

Manoj: Shush… Don't say a word. Better to tell the truth or else you don't know me.

Dr. Somai: Okay, okay. I am saying, please don't kill me. Please.

Manoj: This was too easy, Santosh. Let's sit.

Dr. Somai: I don't have a degree or B.A.M.S. I was just a janitor in a hospital. Mr. Sisodia once asked me to provide a steroid illegally and I helped him.

Santosh: Can't you say no to them.

Dr. Somai: He had a gun, and the point was my head, that's why. Later, he always came in hospital gate and asked me for steroid. I gave him two for a day.

Manoj: Then, how come this clinic?

Dr. Somai: Mr. Sisodia bought this place. He told me that I helped him so well and gifted me to start a new journey. I told him that I don't have a degree, but they arrange fake degrees and hang here. Also, I am a doctor so I can keep any drug in the name of medicine. And they both were big names in the state so they also assured me that no one would be harmed.

Manoj: Oh. I am sorry but I can. They both died last night, and your statement is recorded so that from now, you are demote to prisoner. Your license will be canceled which is already fake, running this fake clinic in the last four years and supplying illegal medicines without prior prescription. You will spend the rest of your life in jail Dr. Somai.

Dr. Somai started crying and felt guilty about whatever he had done in his life. Manoj and Santosh left at wine shop.

**

Santosh and Manoj arrived at wine shop.

Manoj: What do you have?

Badrinath: We have all the brands sirs. Brandy, scotch, whiskey, rum, vodka. What do you want sir?

Manoj: We want something else. What's your name?

Badrinath: Badrinath sir. We have imported brands too. You just say your name.

Manoj: I don't want that. I want something else. Santosh, what was the name of the steroid? Anabolic something? Santosh, what Dr. Somai said?

After hearing this, Badrinath got curious. He felt sweaty.

Manoj: What happened? Don't worry. We are Police Inspectors, but we take it too. Just give me one pill and I will leave.

Badrinath hesitated to say something.

Badrinath: Sir! I don't know what you are talking about. We only sell alcohol, nothing else. Maybe you have misunderstood something.

Manoj: Okay, then. We will discuss it in the police station.

Badrinath was afraid and tried to run from the backside of the store. Manoj and Santosh both ran after him for a long and caught him. They all felt breathless. They took a breath.

Manoj: You run so fast Badri. How many times have you got caught?
Santosh: You ran so fast that I thought you just broke Usain Bolt's record. You should run a race. You will bring gold medal for India.
Manoj: He can't run more, Santosh. Put him in a cell.

**

Manoj and Santosh took Badrinath to the Police Station and put him in a cell. Santosh started making a FIR against him. Later, Manoj and Santosh took him for an interrogation. He brought a stick and a plastic bag with him.
Manoj: So, I think you know what I am going to do. My questions, reactions, results. So, without wasting my precious time, start talking.
Badrinath: No, no. I will tell you everything. Mr. Sisodia helped me to open that shop. He was the one who import illegal alcohol and drugs. I am innocent sir, please let me go. I will not sell illegal things.
Manoj: How do you know Mr. Sisodia?
Badrinath: Years ago, I was accused of drug supplying, he saved me from that case and asked me to do whatever he will say. That is why I sold them and for more money I sold them to other people. Mr. Sisodia does not know about it.
Manoj: You were and now, you will never be going to sell either liquor or drug. Tell me one thing. Did Mr. Jain and Mr. Sisodia come to your shop last night?
Badrinath: Yes sir. They came for Steroid. They both visit every weekend.

Manoj: Every weekend. But the CM said Mr. Jain was in rehab for two years. Did Mr. Jain also take that?

Badrinath: You are right. For two years, my worker delivers those drugs to Mr. Jain at rehab. After that, they both came to my shop directly. I have been supplying them for more than ten years. But from now on I will not.

Manoj: It means Mr. Jain was never recovered from drug addiction. And all the relatives thought he was a good human being. Did he ever ask for a prostitute?

Badrinath: Many times. But that was not my business and never will. I only gave him the contact numbers of girls, nothing else.

Manoj: What was the age of the girls you used to send? Any below eighteen?

Badrinath: No, never. I accept that I sold the illegal drugs, but I never done this irrational thing.

Manoj: Okay. Have you ever seen an abnormal activity behind Mr. Jain or Mr. Sisodia?

Badrinath: Abnormal activity?

Manoj: Have you ever noticed them that they were scared, or someone was following them?

Badrinath: They weren't but one man came at me to ask about them two weeks ago. Once, Mr. Jain was so tired and stressed that they shouted at me and broke some bottles of my shop. That man came to me and asked about incidence. He was just asking as a normal human being, so I did not inform Mr. Jain.

Manoj: Santosh, check his CCTV.

Badrinath: We don't have CCTV at the shop sir. As we are doing illegal business and the shop is named after two mafia or politicians, no one ever tried to rob, steal, or do anything. We have a CCTV but that one was only for show and to scare people.

Manoj: Wow. How can we get him? How has he looked? What was he asking about?

Badrinath: I don't remember his face. There were lots of customer visits in a day, so it is impossible to remember. But he looked so gentle person.

***

Unknown: By the way, who was he?

Badrinath: You don't know him? Everyone here knows him. He was my regular customer; his name is Mr. Jain.

Unknow: Mr. Jain? That Politician and Mafia, right? What is he doing here?

Badrinath: He is not a mafia. He is a good human being. He helped me a lot to start this business. He can break all the bottles in this shop and still I can't say anything to him. He will come in a few minutes and give me money for all this broken bottle.

After a few minutes, Mr. Jain came.

Mr. Jain: Look Badri, I'm sorry for your loss. Take this money and don't forget to deliver a parcel.

Unknown: You told the truth. He is a good person. Where is he going?

Badrinath: At his mansion. He has a very big mansion in Noida's sector 1. I went there so many times for dinner. He is a good person. Wait, who are you? What do you want? You don't look like you are from here.

Unknown: No thanks but, I don't drink. I am a doctor by profession. I can't tolerate violation and seen you in such a condition, so I came. I am from Bhopal. Okay, just take care.

***

Badrinath: We talked this much, and he left.

Manoj: Bhopal? Does he say his name? Any other details?

Badrinath: No sir. He left after saying that.

Manoj: Can you identify or sketch his face?

Badrinath: No. There were lots of people who came to ask for address, bottles, some of them argue, etc. But I will try if I see him in public. I will go back to my shop, and I will let you know if I see him again.

Manoj: No. You are not going anywhere. Santosh, put him in cell.

A constable came and asked them to check the TV. CM took Mr. Jain and Mr. Sisodia's body in public. Their bodies were covered with white cloth.

**

CM: Jai hind. All of you know the highlights of today's topic. In Nine moths Two Rape, three rapists are dead, and One Victim murdered after rape. Mr. Jain and Mr. Sisodia were one of those rapists who tried on my granddaughter. These are Mr. Jain and Mr. Sisodia.

CM signaled the security guard to remove the clothes. Both were hung with wooden table vertically and naked. People were shocked after seeing such kind of act. This action was telecast live. Everyone in the state is watching at home.

CM: They both were dead when the police arrived. Currently nobody knows who killed them but whoever it was, I want to tell him Thank you. Sometimes laws could not show their power, so people like you must show in the shadow.

Reporter: What exactly had done there? Can you please brief me about it? And what are you going to do with their bodies?

CM: All your questions will be answered. A few days ago, my granddaughter turned seventeen years. It was her birthday, and we organized a party with her friends and their families at my mansion. But these two rapists kidnapped her, took her into their mansion, bitten her face so badly, brutally raped and inserted a metal rode inside her.

CM's eyes filled with pain and anger as soon as she spoke. She took a breath and controlled her emotions.

CM: Who does that? Human, right? How does the person's lust increase so much that he rapes someone. If the rapist does not get that much satisfaction they want, then they put a hand, a bottle and now even a rod inside them. Seeing such people, I wish I was an animal. People like these have questioned being human.

CM felt like crying. Her PA brought a water bottle and handkerchief for her.

CM: I saw my granddaughter today, and I felt so scared to look at her. Even whenever her face comes in front my eyes, I get very scared. I was always thinking about protecting this state but could not save anyone. Even my granddaughter. At that night don't know when savior or killer whatever you all say to him came and killed them both. But he could not save my granddaughter. I know he tried to save my granddaughter too, but he could not save her. He Punished both and result is Infront of you. As you can see, their private parts were cut in half. So, out there any of trying to rape or even think then you will face the same. We will not be going to kill you, but you will live your whole life out in the world like this.

CM signaled again security guard. He brought a torch and fire them both Infront of national television.

CM: I didn't do this because they are dead. If they were alive, I will burn to the death the same way. I want to feel the pain that my... We don't need their bones. Also, according to rituals, we don't want to pollute the river by throwing their ashes in it. We don't need this kind of person who kidnap and rape minors or girls or women. This march is the warning for the people who is thinking or had done rape. I promise, if you found guilty, your each second of breath feels like hell. They don't deserve to live, but we will; I will let them live like they never want to. Committee will make a new rule, new team, and new division for all the rape cases. I request you all for the peace of my granddaughter's soul and in the memory of the dead, we will do a candle march tomorrow evening. Jai hind.

**

Santosh: Everything will change from now on, I guess. Women and girls can freely live and roam even in night. They will have powers too like men.

Manoj smiled a little.

Manoj: Women already have that power. But after this statement, most of the women will take it wrong way. Do you know about feminists?
Santosh: Yes. What…
Manoj: I mean that, ask any women in the country about women empowerment. What is the thing that women fighting for? Many women will say only about job, money, they don't need men to live, etc. but less of them will say about this incidence. In this life, women have powers to do anything, still, they fight for useless rights and don't know why. If men earn something, he is earning for the family; if women earn something, she is earning for herself.
Santosh: Not all the women do this sir.
Manoj: Yes. And not all the men do this Santosh. There are so many women out there who will take this power to wrong way. Let's see where the path will take us. And we must find that murderer too.

**

In an empty room, a satellite non-tracker phone rang on the door. Someone came and picked me up with fear. He was sweating.
Person One: Who?
Person Two: I don't know who done this boss. Because of Mr. Jain and Mr. Sisodia's death, supply almost stopped in the city. There are police everywhere in the city. Some of our packets had been caught by the police. Some of them were our person so we still have 30% packets available, but we need more for our guests. How will we manage?
Person One took a second to think and deep breath.

4.24 - A Date & A Time

Person One: What Chennai is doing?

Person Two: Don't know. It has been a long time since we had business with him.

Person One: Ask him to handle it for a few months. I will be back in the town, and I will handle it. Till then, throw the money at everyone who tries to stop us. I want no lose in this business. Got it?

Person Two: Yes sir. I will. We will wait for you, our king Mr....

Person One: Shh… No name on the call. I don't want to lose my positive reputation in the market. I will see you soon, buddy.

*****

We fail as a human.

People teach their child that woman is a goddess and Laxmi of house. But some people forgot to teach how to respect, and how to behave.

People ask their girls not to stay outside till late night, but man and boys can stay, drink and drive, tease, and any "Fun" activity. We all are the responsible not to make our society safe. Bad touches should not only for girls to stay safe. Education system can teach the circumstances, safety awareness, and sex education into schools. But people shame to talk about and just say "good touch, bad touch and don't wear short dress."

It is not helpful for a 1-year-old baby who wear diapers, and 10-year-old boy raped her.
It is not helpful for a 10-year-old girl who is mute, and a 20-year-old boy who is her friend.

These are just an example as we know how cruel human can be. 40-year-old raped 1-year-old. 15-year-old raped 60-year-old, etc.

It is not about dress she wears, late night travelling she do, live alone to build her empire, or profession and more.
If this goes on, then people will scare to even talk with other and survive only for safety.

4.24 - A Date & A Time

Chapter 3

Don't ever feel Guilty. The universe will give you a time to heal from it.

4.24 - A Date & A Time

Chennai. 12th May 2016

At home, more than thirty people gathered in a hall. They hold Valeri, Chopper knife, dagger, and coconut knife in hand. They were waiting for someone. After a few minutes, Mr. Chaitanya came from upstairs.

■■

Mr. Chaitanya was a 55-year-old mafia of a whole south region. He was a one of the biggest drug dealers in India. Police, politicians, no one has the courage to stop him or catch him. Although, Politicians don't want to because he bribes them weekly. There was a time when Mr. Chaitanya and Mr. Luthra were doing business together. Before Mr. Jain and Mr. Sisodia, Mr. Chaitanya helped Mr. Luthra to place his business in the North region. The illegal business of supplying drugs. Mr. Chaitanya had power to control whole India, but he had interest in girls. Not to marry or live a life with them, he sale and supply girls to other countries. Many people registered complaints against him, but no one can catch him. Except one.

■■

Mr. Chaitanya: Vanakkam, my friends. Yesterday, I received a call from my dearest friend Luthra.
He took mobile from his pocket and put it on the table. Everyone felt joy and smiled after hearing this.
Mr. Chaitanya: He wanted to do business again with us. The offer is for the whole North region. He asked me 'Do you want to do business with me?'

He was silent for a while. Everyone smiled and waited for his reply.

Raja: And what did you say?

Mr. Chaitanya smiled and shouted.

Mr. Chaitanya: I was, I am, I will be the only King of India.

Everyone felt joy and started chattering Mr. Chaitanya's name as 'Anna'.

Mr. Chaitanya: Okay, okay. Relax. Inform all the suppliers, the order of all drugs is increased to ten times. You all know how to supply it to the North area.

Raja: But Anna. It has been so many years since we did business out of the South. We must manage police, highways, airports, and all.

Mr. Chaitanya: Raja! People say that a human being has 7 births. If I shoot you, will you forget to live in the next life? This question should not come again. We are coming after many years; it will cost a little money, but we will have that power again. You all know what to do and how to tackle situations. Luthra will arrive soon for a meeting. Till then, we will supply continuously in the North. I want his all friends to be happy because if his friends are happy Mr. Luthra will be happy.

Everyone was so happy and hugged each other. Later, they all went to work. Mr. Chaitanya took mobile from table and dialed a number.

Mr. Chaitanya: Srinu. My friend. My brother.

Mr. Srinivasan: Hey, Chintu. How are you? After a long time. How are you? What happened? Are your businesses, okay?

■■

Mr. Srinivasan was a top named businessman in South region. His businesses were in almost all the fields and his income was ten times higher of India's richest person Mr. Luthra, but still can't be the richest man in world because he donated his 80% of income in poor people, old age home and animal welfare. He was Mr. Chaitanya's childhood friend. He knows what his friend is doing and never supported him in his business, but their friendship bond was too strong.

■■

Mr. Chaitanya: White marble. Do you remember?
Mr. Srinivasan: What is White marble? Are you going to sell White marbles now? Should I give you my companies franchise and best location with…
Mr. Chaitanya: Ille, Srinu. A few years ago, I told you the same and you asked me the same. What is this? You should eat almonds Srinu.
Mr. Srinivasan: I am old, Chintu. I am eating, but there are so many things to remember in business. Tell me what is White marble?
Mr. Chaitanya: Green signal for white marble.
Mr. Srinivasan was shocked after hearing this. He was drinking water, and he split it from his mouth.
Mr. Srinivasan: What? Chintu, look. Don't do this. I am telling you; you are going to end yourself. You had done earlier this too and you know that I was right, and I am right too.
Mr. Chaitanya: Chill, Srinu. This time I will not repeat the same mistake. I got caught twelve years ago because of Shailesh Khare. He was dead the very second day

with the help of Mr. Luthra. Now, Shailesh is not alive, so I can do my business.

Mr. Srinivasan: Shailesh is dead but what if someone like Shailesh caught you?

Mr. Chaitanya: So, what? History will repeat itself again, my friend. The hand of Mr. Luthra is on my head. If someone interferes in our business, then he will suffer the same. Let's meet tonight at my villa. It has been a long time since we sat together and drank a small whiskey.

Mr. Srinivasan: We will surely meet tonight. But look, Chintu. I warn you again. Please don't make the same mistake again. Whatever you have done in your past life, you must suffer, and you will suffer.

Mr. Srinivasan was trying to believe in his sayings, but Mr. Chaitanya could not stand any more. He shouted at him.

Mr. Chaitanya: Hey, Srinu. Stop repeating nonsense things. I heard you and I ignored you, okay? If you want to talk about something else, then come, otherwise go to hell.

Mr. Chaitanya hung up the call. He smiled a little as he knew that Mr. Srinivasan would join his success. Mr. Chaitanya went to his room.

**

From 31st August 2016, Mr. Chaitanya started supplying drugs to North Region. In these two months, he contacted almost all police Inspectors and bribed them not to interfere in their business. Mr. Chaitanya arranged many kinds of drugs, cocaine, and LSD. Yet, they don't know who is supplying in the

North region, and Mr. Chaitanya won't like it. He wanted his name and fear in the North.

**

At Manoj's police station, he came in the cabin and shouted loud.
Manoj: Santosh?
Santosh: Jai hind, sir. What happened?
Manoj: There are kids around fifteen years old, who bought drugs from somewhere. Who is supplying and people are buying freely like a toffee. What is happening in this city?
Santosh: Sir… It… The thing is…
Manoj: What? Why are you afraid? Who is he? What is his name?
Santosh: We don't know the name yet but, almost all the Inspector and Inspectors were bribed. We can say the whole city is under its control.
Manoj: What nonsense is this? He got famous without a name. And people are already afraid of him.
Santosh: It is the truth, sir. No one is more dangerous than those who become famous without their name. Everyone knows that someone is supplying drugs but don't know Who? Where? How? Nobody even wanted to know because they are getting what they want. Everyone is getting everything, so does it is important who is giving?
Manoj: So, what? It is our duty to find out and put him in a cell.
Santosh: Do you think we can catch him and put him in cell? Look into your past, not a year but a month or a two. There was not a single trace of the drug. Now,

he is openly selling drugs, and no one can do anything. Still, we are trying to catch him, sir.

Santosh left from cabin and Manoj sat about thinking.

**

Till November 2016, young generation and whoever was intoxicated, taking different drugs but still nobody knows the main supplier. Nobody even cares except Manoj. He and his team took three months to find out who is supplying it. Because of Alok's rape case and suicide, checking got strict. Most of the youngsters were either school or college students who took drugs. Every road, entrance in the city, bus, train and even in mall and theatre, police checked every single person. The government also added a mental health section for students and workers in schools and offices. They diagnosed by only specialist for each person by conversation. It helped so many people like youngsters and working people to release their stress. They used to take drug just to relieve from stress but because of psychiatrist.

■■■

By February 2017, the supply of drugs had half in the North region. Mr. Chaitanya was not happy about seeing this. Mr. Luthra was sadder than him. He called Mr. Chaitanya to discuss it.

Mr. Luthra: Chaitanya, I trusted you. I give you permission to do business with me, but you lose. It was going well till February. I guess someone else can do a better job than you.

Mr. Chaitanya: Ille, sir. I know I made some mistakes, but I can fix them. Just give me some more time. There is a saying that 'The day was bad, not life'. Please give me one last chance so I will do business like before. North will fire again.

Mr. Luthra: I am coming India in mid-June. You only have one month. Till then you keep my guests happy, I will be happy. If you haven't done anything by then, I won't be able to do anything for you either. I think you must have understood my point, Mr. Rajappa Chaitanya.

Mr. Chaitanya was afraid. He knew that if he could not do it then no one could save him from the police, law, and state. All the evidence will turn against him, and he will either get killed or put in the cell for rest of his life.

Mr. Chaitanya: Y... Yes, sir. I will.

Mr. Luthra: And yes. What about your old business? Are you still doing it or not?

Mr. Chaitanya: Old business? Do you mean Hudugi?

Mr. Luthra: Yes.

Mr. Chaitanya: Yes, I am. What do you want sir? Cinnapilla, yuvakudu, patadi, VIP? Just say sir. We have all the verities to taste.

Mr. Luthra: Hmm. I will tell you later.

**

Mr. Luthra hung up the call. Mr. Chaitanya called Raja in the hall.

Mr. Chaitanya: What is happening in the North? Why Mr. Luthra's guests did not receive packages there? Why? What is the reason?

Raja: Few months ago, CM's granddaughter was kidnapped and brutally raped.

4.24 - A Date & A Time

Mr. Chaitanya: I know about it. Mr. Jain & Mr. Sisodia died that is why I got an opportunity to do business with Mr. Luthra. Tell me something else.

Raja: After that, we cracked a big deal there. Most of youngsters and working people bought drugs. But after the suicide of a college boy, school, colleges, and companies recruited psychologists to reduce stress.

Mr. Chaitanya: And?

Raja: Everybody went to therapy and people stopped buying drugs to reduce stress.

Mr. Chaitanya: Is this an excuse or a reason to not do business?

Raja: Rea…

Mr. Chaitanya: Shut up. This… Shall I tell Mr. Luthra that 'Sir, actually everyone is taking psychology therapy that is why people are not buying drugs.' Is this the reason? You are not selling; people are buying. We are not salespeople that we go to person to person and advertise 'Sir, this is LSD. It will release your hormones and make you feel better.' We are not salesmen. We don't find them, they find us. What about other places?

Raja: Right now, we have limited places to supply.

Mr. Chaitanya: Why? We are giving money to so many bars and clubs, then why we can't have a business?

Raja: Police…

Mr. Chaitanya: Oh, God. Do one thing, book a ticket to Delhi. It has been a long time since I visited Delhi. Book today's night flight. You and I are going. Inform Raghu about it.

Mr. Chaitanya leaves for his room for packing. Raja went to the airport to book a flight.

**

The other side, Manoj was trying to get a hint of a supplier in the city. For some time, he was buying drugs from a dealer, so that he could become a regular customer, and started becoming friend. He got some news from Santosh that the person was in a bar. Manoj went at the bar. He was sitting on a chair with empty glass in his hand.
Manoj: Hey, buddy. How are you? Why your glass is empty?
Raghuraj: Hey, Manoj. I'm not good. Business is not doing well. I'm sorry but I don't have anything to give today.
Manoj: Oh. But don't worry, I will buy you a drink tonight. Tonight, we both will get drunk.
Raghuraj: No, you drink. I am not making profit in my business right now. On top of that alcohol addiction is expensive if you want to get high quickly.
Manoj: Come on. It has been a long time since I took a delivery from you. Tonight's drinks are on me.
Manoj called waiter to take the order.
Manoj: Say, what do you want?
Raghuraj: Umm… It is on you. Order whatever you want bro.
Manoj: Okay. Bring one JD Black. Tonight, we both end the full bottle. And with water or a cold drink?
Raghuraj: Cold drink will be preferable.
Manoj: Did you hear what brother said? Go and get it.
Raghuraj: Sounds good.
The waiter goes and brings a whiskey bottle with two glasses, cold drink, ice cubes and chips as a snack.

Raghuraj: What do you do?
Manoj got curious for a while.
Manoj: I have a fruit stall near Lal Darwaja.
Raghuraj: Who is in your house? Your father, mother, wife, or kids?
Manoj got emotional.
Manoj: My father got killed twelve years ago. At that time, I was studying, and my age was twenty. He got into a fight with someone and they... I saw my father's dying Infront of me. There was a knife inserted in his chest, bullets, and blood on his cloth. He held my hand while taking his last breath. I don't know what to do, and there is no one to help us. He was my guardian, my hero. After some time, the police came and took him to a hospital. But due to excessive blood loss, he could not survive. My mother went into a coma as she could not handle my father's death. I left to study to take care of my mother. I wanted to cry, scream loudly but there was no one who could handle my mother. That is why I built myself different. After a few months of my father's death, my mother also passed away.
Manoj got emotional and cried. Raghuraj also got emotional, and he supported Manoj by giving him a handkerchief and a whiskey.
Raghuraj: I... I am sorry for your loss, brother. Take a drink. When you started taking drugs?
Manoj: After a few months of my mother's death, I met a person who become friend. He gave me strength and drugs to forget the past. That is how started taking it. I told you too much about myself, now tell me yourself. Is Tom your real name?

Raghuraj: Our kind of people's work is so dangerous that we can't make friends or tell our real name. There are some people who will help at your lowest, but you will also never know when they will run and put you in the mud. You will move your hands and legs, but you will not be able to come out of that mud. No one will help. Then, you must control your mind, and do it yourself. I became a drug dealer just to earn money. I am addicted to money not drugs. I am just a drug dealer.

Manoj: Just? You are a savior for so many people. Who are in stress don't want to live in this cruel world, you are giving them medicine. You are a doctor, brother.

Raghuraj smiled a little.

Manoj: But all of this, you did not tell your name.

Raghuraj: I told you, brother. We can't say our name. I have some principles too.

Manoj: Okay, alright. Do you have anything right now? I am craving it.

Raghuraj: I am so sorry, brother. I have empty pockets, I told you. I can't help you today.

Manoj: Oh, God. I want that kick. And even you did not take drug. I I know drug dealers can be so innocent and gentle. By the way, if you don't have a phone, then is there anyone else you can help? Can I buy directly from the main supplier?

Raghuraj found something wrong. He looked at Manoj suspiciously.

Raghuraj: Who are you?

Manoj: What… What do you mean by who I am?

4.24 - A Date & A Time

Raghuraj: You asked for direct contact of a supplier, not any other dealer. I have been selling for the past four years, and no one asked me this. Are you a Police Inspector? Tell me who you are.

Raghuraj got angry and scared at the same time. He did not want to get caught, and Manoj also don't want to lose his trust.

Manoj: Brother, I told you who I am. A fruit seller, nothing else. There is a reason behind this question. I have been buying from you every day for the last six to seven months. You are always alone. I had never seen anyone else. No friends, family, no one. Look around you. I understand that in your business, nothing is like friendship. Look at your mobile, you are still using that 1990s keypad mobile. How many contacts do you have? Okay, I am asking what you want me to ask, so do you have any other dealer contact number?

Raghuraj thought for a while, and poured almost half of a glass whiskey and drank neat. Manoj played physiologically and gained his trust again. Raghuraj felt guilty and without saying anything, he made a drink for Manoj.

Raghuraj: I am sorry, brother. You are right. I am all alone. I tried to fit in smugglers but could not. They are way different than I am. My target was to make money not to take drugs. I have other dealers contact, wrote it down.

Manoj wanted to know direct supplier, but he took other dealer numbers so that he would catch them and put in cell.

Manoj: Thank you, brother. I am dealing with them because you don't have any. I will always buy from you only.
Raghuraj: Sure, sure.

**

After a few hours of emptying two bottles, Manoj felt little bit high. He was conscious. But Raghuraj A.K.A Tom was gone. Manoj started asking questions what answers he was looking for.
Manoj: Hey… Hey. Get up. Tell me, who is supplying drugs in North? What is his name?
Manoj slapped him a little and threw water on his face, but he drank so much that he could not have any sense what he could say.
Raghuraj: I… I don't have any drug right now. I will give it to you tomorrow.
Manoj: Hey. I want the name of the main dealer. What is his name?
Raghuraj: I gave you the number of many dealers, brother. But next time buy it from me. Thank you for the party, brother.
Manoj: What is his name?
Raghuraj: Brother, I am not Tom. My real name is Raghuraj.
Manoj slapped him again.
Raghuraj: No, mummy. I will not go to school today. I have a stomachache.
Manoj: Okay. What is your teacher's name? What is his contact number? I must tell him that you are ill, right? Come on, give me his details.
A dealer: Ch… Cha… Chaitanya.

4.24 - A Date & A Time

Manoj was shocked. After hearing the name, all his intoxication went away. He took A dealer's mobile and found Chaitanya's number. Manoj messaged his number to Santosh. He also took Raghuraj and drove to the police station. He called Santosh while driving.

Manoj: Santosh, I sent you a number. Try to get as many details as you can. If I am thinking and it's the same, then I am going to kill this man at any cost.

Santosh: What happened?

Manoj: No questions Santosh. Just do as I say.

Santosh started getting details of contact. But he got nothing.

**

After a few minutes, Manoj arrived in police station.

Manoj: Have you got anything?

Santosh: No, sir. This sim card was activated a week ago.

Manoj: What? Damn it. There is a person sleeping in my car, get him.

Santosh ran and brought Raghuraj.

Santosh: Who is he?

Manoj: A drug dealer. He gave me more contact details. By tomorrow morning at 11, I want all these people in the cell. Wake him up and bring him into the room.

Santosh picked Raghuraj and brought him to the Interrogation room. He tied him to a chair. He also brought a stick, plastic bag, Water, and shocker. Manoj throws water on Raghuraj face. Raghuraj fell unconscious.

Raghuraj: Manoj, what are you doing?

Manoj: Inspector Manoj. I am not your friend.

Raghuraj got scared and begged to let him go.

Raghuraj: Hey, Manoj. I mean sir. Please let me go. I gave you drugs to release stress. I can also give you money. Tell me how much you want? Ten, Twenty, Fifty? Just tell me numbers.

Santosh: Hey, shut up. He is not a person you meet every day.

Manoj: Okay, Raghuraj. I will give you freedom. Just tell me about Chaitanya. Who is he?

Raghuraj: Cha... Chaitanya? Who is Chaitanya? I don't know anybody named Chaitanya.

Mano held a stick and started hitting on his Knee and Shin. Raghuraj started crying.

Raghuraj: Stop, no. Please. I don't know anyone.

Manoj: Just tell me about him. Who is Chaitanya?

Manoj hitting his leg continuously. Santosh got shocked while seeing Manoj's this form. Manoj's eyes being red. Blood came from Raghuraj's leg. Manoj stopped a little. Raghuraj was crying continuously.

Raghuraj: Please, let me go. I don't know who he is. Where he is.

Manoj: I am telling you, Raghuraj. I will give you freedom, just tell me about Chaitanya. Where is he? What is he doing? How? Who is protecting him?

Raghuraj: Manoj. Sir, Manoj. I don't know anything you are talking about. I never even mentioned Chaitanya's name.

Manoj: Raghuraj, a person speaks the truth only twice. When he is very angry, and when he is drunk. Now, tell me where he is, I will let you go.

Raghuraj: I am still telling you. I don't know who he is, where he is. I really don't know.

Manoj could not stand. He throws sticks and puts plastic bag on his head. Raghuraj could not breathe.

Santosh: What are you doing sir? He will die.

Santosh tried to stop Manoj. He held his hand but, Manoj pushed him. Manoj was not in control at all. Raghuraj was trying to survive and breathe.

Santosh: Sir, he is saying something.

Manoj stopped and removed bag from his head.

Manoj: Tell me about Chaitanya.

Raghuraj: I am telling you everything. Please, please give me water.

Manoj throws water on his face. Raghuraj breathes heavily.

Manoj: Want more. First, tell me all the details about Chaitanya.

Raghuraj: Chaitanya, South region's biggest mafia. His full name is Rajappa Chaitanya. No one can even touch him. He was smuggled girls and women from whole India to foreign countries. Few months back, someone called and deal with him to smuggle drugs in whole North region. I was smuggling minor girls for him. After the CM's speech, it was hard to do that business. That is why he ordered me to smuggle drugs.

Manoj: Where is he?

Raghuraj: Chennai.

Manoj: Santosh, let us go to Chennai.

Raghuraj: There is no point going there.

Manoj: You just said he is in Chennai. I will go there and kill there. I want to see fear of death in his eyes.

Raghuraj laughed.
Manoj: Why are you laughing?
Raghuraj: You can't kill him. You can't even touch him. Twelve years ago, a police Inspector had done the same. Went to Chennai to catch him. When he arrived his city, he got killed. This time, you just don't want to go there, he is coming to Delhi next month to meet with power.
Manoj: Who?
Raghuraj: Luthra. The biggest and richest businesspeople in India. If Chaitanya has Luthra's support, you can't do anything to him. You can't touch him. Let's assume that even if you catch him, Luthra will do the same with you that happened with policeman twelve years ago.
Manoj could not control himself. He took his gun from his back and shot Raghuraj in his forehead in anger. Santosh was shocked.
Santosh: Sir, what have you done! What happened to you? Who is Chaitanya? Why had you become so angry after hearing this?
Manoj kept silent. He only wants Rajappa Chaitanya. After a few minutes, Manoj went to his cabin and started crying. Santosh tried to clear the room. Later, he went at Manoj's cabin.
Santosh: Sir, are you okay?
Manoj wiped his tears and drank water.
Manoj: Raghuraj was a drug dealer, and kidnap young girls for smuggling. During the interrogation, Raghuraj tried to fight with us. He stole a gun from my pocket. After snatching from his hand, he took handcuff and

attacked me. He also tries to run from room, and during a fight, I had to shoot him.

Manoj took handcuff from droor, and hurt himself on his forearms, shoulders, and neck. Santosh was so confused, he had so many questions to ask, but Manoj was not in the phase to answer any of this. He stood for a while and left the room.

Manoj: Santosh.

Santosh: Yes, sir.

Manoj: Get every possible detail of Rajappa Chaitanya. His business, locations, and all. We don't have much time. I want him dead at any cost.

Santosh: Yes, sir.

Santosh started finding details of Mr. Chaitanya. Santosh got some news via internet and local police station that he is still kidnapping and selling girls and women to foreign.

**

Manoj was sitting on a chair in his cabin and constantly looking at Mr. Chaitanya's photo. In one day, Santosh prepared a complete file of Mr. Chaitanya's illegal businesses and placed on Manoj's desk.

Santosh: File is ready sir.

Manoj didn't respond. Santosh was waiting of his response.

Santosh: Any idea how we can catch him?

Manoj smiled and took his mobile phone and called Anaya.

Manoj: Anaya. Are you busy right now?

Anaya: Yes, working on something. Tell me what happened.

Manoj: I need your help. Can you meet me at Café in the evening?
Anaya: Sure. You can tell me now if it is urgent.
Manoj: I will tell you all the things in the evening.

**

In the evening, Manoj and Anaya met at the Café.
Anaya: Tell me, what happened?
Manoj: There is a person who is selling drugs as well as kidnapping minor girls and women and selling to other countries. I want your help to catch him.
Anay: Who is he? What can I do? What is your plan?
Manoj: His name is Rajappa Chaitanya. He is in the South region's mafia. He is coming in a few weeks to deal with Mr. Luthra.
Anaya: Wait. Mr. Luthra? The richest person? Why would he deal with Mr. Luthra?
Manoj: Because Mr. Luthra informed or ordered Mr. Chaitanya to supply drugs in North region. He is the main villain in this whole game.
Anaya: Then, we should directly catch Mr. Luthra.
Manoj: No. I will catch him but after killing Mr. Chaitanya. My target is Mr. Chaitanya right now and I need your support.
Anaya: Okay. But how can I help you with this?
Manoj: Mr. Chaitanya kidnap and supply girls & women to another region. He is coming in Delhi in few weeks. There will a party with lots of girls, you know… Party. Enjoyment.
Anaya: Okay, I got it. Then?
Manoj: Mr. Chaitanya and Mr. Luthra are also a big… You know what I mean.

4.24 - A Date & A Time

Anaya: Okay. Then?
Manoj: If we both can go to that party, and somehow you become the victim. Then we can complete our job.
Anaya: Victim? Like you want me to seduce Mr. Chaitanya, take him to the room, and there you will kill him. Is this your plan? What if he catches us? What if you could not come on time? How will we enter the party?
Manoj: Shush… I know there are so many questions but believe me.

Manoj holds Anaya's hand and look into her eyes for a few seconds. There was a spark between them. Suddenly, Anaya took her hand back.

Anaya: Okay. Umm… We will. We will be going to do it. Why don't we just catch him and let the law do the work?
Manoj: Someone tried twelve years ago. But he failed. I don't want to take the risk again.

Anaya and Manoj sat for a while.

**

Manoj tried to contact a person who arranges the party and let them enter. Somehow, Manoj manages to get permission without knowing either Mr. Luthra or Mr. Chaitanya. Manoj was sitting on his chair.
Santosh: Sir, what if you could not save Anaya?
Manoj: I will, Santosh. And I have to. There is no other option.

**

On the other side, Mr. Chaitanya was ready to take a flight, and got the news about Raghuraj.
Raja: Anna. Some police Inspector killed Raghu.

Mr. Chaitanya got angry.
Mr. Chaitanya: What? Who? What is his name?
Raja: His name is Manoj Khare. Don't know how he caught him, but he shot him in the head.
Mr. Chaitanya: Khare? Get all the details of that Inspector. Tell others to arrange it for me. Something is not right.
Raja got the whole data of Manoj within a minute. They also got his photo. Another way, Mr. Chaitanya's goon arranged a big Villa for the party. They shared the address of that location in no time.
Mr. Chaitanya: Sir, all the arrangements are ready. Our car will be there to pick you up from the airport.
Mr. Luthra: No. Media knows my car, number, and all. You just send a driver to my office and my people will take care of it.

**

It was 15th June 2016; in the evening Mr. Luthra came to Delhi. Media already knows because he was the richest and biggest person in India. Media shows the live telecast of Mr. Luthra's visit India on national television. It became hard to go to the party and meet Mr. Chaitanya. He entered a blue sedan, and a white sedan followed him. Media started following him. There was a tunnel on the way to the hotel. Both the cars drive beside each other and both doors opened. Mr. Luthra jumped from one car to another, and blue sedan went in right which media followed. While the white Sedan which Mr. Luthra presented were went to the left. Mr. Luthra took his mobile and called Mr. Chaitanya.

Mr. Luthra: I am on my way.
Mr. Chaitanya: Okay, sir. We are waiting. Raja Mr. Luthra is coming. All the arrangements have been made properly, haven't they?
Raja: All okay sir. Don't worry.

**

Manoj was present at the party as waiter, and Anaya will arrive as a dancer. All the waiters were wearing masks. Anaya was getting ready at the hotel arranged by Mr. Chaitanya's goon.
Raja: Are you all ready or not? Come on, our boss is waiting to see all of you.
Anaya was scared. She was neither a fighter nor in the police. Still, she was ready to fight for the country. She went to the hall with other dancers. They all started dancing Infront of Mr. Chaitanya's guest. Anaya felt shy to do this. Mr. Luthra arrived at the party. Mr. Chaitanya kissed on Mr. Luthra's hand to show respect.
Mr. Chaitanya: Stop the music. My dearest friend, we have our beloved guest Mr. Luthra in the house. Please clap for him.
Mr. Luthra does not like whatever he was doing.
Mr. Luthra: Stop doing this. I only came here to discuss business with you. Not this.
Mr. Chaitanya: Sorry, sir. Hey, play the music. Is this okay sir?
Mr. Luthra was irritated with Mr. Chaitanya's behavior. Mr. Chaitanya offered him to sit on the main couch. Raja asked Manoj to stay with Mr. Luthra and give a great hospitality. He brought fine whiskey with a snack.

There was a packet in the tray too. Manoj also don't know what it is.

Mr. Luthra: What is this?

Mr. Chaitanya: This is our specialty. Your mind will blow after taking this, and a beast will come from inside you.

Mr. Luthra: Okay, alright.

Mr. Chaitanya: Tell me, sir. How can I help you?

Mr. Luthra: You are doing nothing for me. I want you to focus on business rather than these things. This party, dancers, what is this?

Mr. Chaitanya: These arrangements are only for you, sir. We have covered almost all the cities in the North. At the start, the business was going too well, but I accepted that later it went slow. But now we are doing very well. The profit is in the bedroom. Whenever you want to leave, my man will put it in your car.

Mr. Luthra: No, don't put anything in my car. Not a single cash, packet of drug or a bottle I want in my car. Not even a smell. You don't know what my reputation in this country is. By the way, how much?

Mr. Chaitanya: One hundred only.

Mr. Luthra smiled a little.

Mr. Luthra: You are doing a good work. Hey, you. Make a hard for Chaitanya.

Mr. Luthra ordered Manoj. Manoj made a hard peg for him.

Mr. Chaitanya: Sir, shall I light a cigarette for you?

Mr. Luthra: Hmm. I feel so empty around me.

Mr. Chaitanya understood and called two dancers.

Mr. Chaitanya: Sure sir. Hey, come here. Give him some comfort please. If you need anything, the waiter is here. If you need more comfort, then…

Mr. Luthra: No, no. Please. Thanks a lot Mr. Chaitanya. I hope we will have a good dela and remain connected in future. And if there is anything goes wrong… You know what I can do.

Mr. Chaitanya was shocked and scared.

Mr. Luthra: I want to spend some time with this princess. Where is my room?

Mr. Chaitanya: First floor right side. Main room is only book for you. All things are available there. If you still need anything, my waiter will be there for your service the whole night.

Mr. Luthra stood up.

Mr. Luthra: Great service Mr. Chaitanya. I will remember this night. And do one thing, before morning, all the money will be delivered to my address. They will handle the rest of it.

Mr. Chaitanya smiled after hearing this. He ordered Manoj to follow Mr. Luthra and take care of him. Manoj followed Mr. Luthra and looked for Anaya. Anaya was standing awkwardly near the guest. Manoj looked at Anaya and signaled her to go to Mr. Chaitanya.

**

Anaya went there and started dancing. Mr. Chaitanya sat on the couch and ordered the waiter to bring a bottle of whiskey, wine, and a special packet. In a few, Mr. Chaitanya grabbed her hand and pulled at him. He started teasing her which Anaya did not like it, but she did too. She stood up and started running towards the room.

Mr. Chaitanya: Raja. Take care of the guest. I am going to enjoy my night.

Mr. Chaitanya also ran towards the room. Manoj don't know what is happening on the ground floor. He waited outside of the room for a while. There was no one else on the floor. After a few minutes, he knocked on the door. A girl opened it.

Manoj: Ma'am, can you please ask sir if he needs something?

Mr. Luthra heard it and shouted.

Mr. Luthra: Hey, don't disturb us. I will tell you if I need something.

That girl closed the door. After a few more minutes, Manoj knocked on the door again. The same girl opened the door.

Manoj: Ma'am, do you need wine or whiskey or anything?

Mr. Luthra got angry and went outside. He grabbed his collar and pushed him.

Mr. Luthra: I told you not to disturb us. Get out of here.

Mr. Luthra went to the room and closed the door.

Manoj ran at the party. He saw Anaya was not there. Raja saw Manoj at the party and went at him.

Raja: Hey, what are you doing? Anna said that you should stay with Mr. Luthra.

Manoj: Actually, he told me to come down and look after Mr. Chaitanya. If he is alright.

Raja: What? I don't believe this.

Manoj: He told me to. That is why I am here. Why would I lie and disrespect the biggest and richest person?
Raja looked at him suspiciously.
Raja: Okay. He is with someone in that room. He is doing good. Okay? Now, go to work.
Manoj: Can I meet him?
Raja: What? Why?
Manoj: Mr. Luthra said to look after Mr. Chaitanya. So, if he himself says that everything is fine and nothing is needed, then I will go to the upper room again.
Raja: Okay, come with me.
Manoj and Raja both went at Mr. Chaitanya's room. Raja knocked at the door, but no one opened the door. Raja felt weird. He knocked again, but no response.
Raja: Why is he not opening the door?
Manoj: Maybe he is asleep?
Raja: No. Go and get the room keys.
Manoj ran and grabbed the keys. Raja opened the door and saw Mr. Chaitanya lying face down on the floor and his leg bleeding. Anaya was crying in the corner. Raja and Manoj were both shocked after seeing this. Raja was about to shout but Manoj tried to chock. Raja tried to resist and removed his mask. Raja could not fight and fainted. Manoj put Raja on the floor and closed the door. Manoj ran towards Anaya. Her clothes were torn and there were some nails scratch marks on her neck and back. Manoj covered her with bedsheet.
Manoj: What happened here?
Anaya was not in the phase to say anything. In the meantime, Mr. Chaitanya woke up. His leg was

bleeding, so he took a pillow, removed his cover, and strapped it on his wound. Mr. Chaitanya saw Manoj's face.

Mr. Chaitanya: Inspector Manoj Khare? How did you enter this party? Hey, anybody. Come here.

Manoj: Music is so loud. No one can hear your voice.

Manoj stood and went at Mr. Chaitanya. He looked at his leg.

Manoj: Is it hurt?

Mr. Chaitanya: No. I feel so good. It is not my blood; it is tomato catchup. What are you asking? She cut my veins or what and I can't feel my leg.

Manoj: Who? Her? She was crying in the corner. There are nail scratches on her body, and you are saying she hurts you? If it is, then great.

Mr. Chaitanya: Believe me. Please call the ambulance or take me to the hospital.

Manoj looked at him and took a gun from his back.

Mr. Chaitanya: Hey, what are you doing? Okay, alright. I am accepting all the crimes I have committed. Please put me in jail. Court will punish me.

Manoj: No, Rajappa Chaitanya. This time the court will not judge you. I know, if I put you in jail then in a few minutes, you will be free. Later, you find me and kill me. I won't make the same mistake my father did.

Mr. Chaitanya laughed.

Mr. Chaitanya: All this planned, right? Manoj Shekhar Khare. I already know about you, your father and the scene that happened twelve years ago. Your father is really a hero, and I am saying this from the bottom of my heart. He is the only one who has that courage to catch me. He had a file against me. He came to Chennai to arrest me, and he completed his task too. But he does not know my power, contacts. He was so happy and left for Delhi. As soon as he reached his home, he got killed. The very next day, on the news it came that a hero was shot dead by Rajappa Chaitanya.

Manoj: How can I forget that day. It has been almost a month since I met with my father because he was busy finding you. When I got a call from him, I was so happy, cherished. When he arrived at home, his face had smile. The difference between us was ten feet. But you shot him in the back. You are not a man; you are a coward. Because neither you nor your men have that courage to shoot from front. He shot three bullets in his back that day. I was shocked after seeing this. I ran towards him, but he fell on the ground. His head was in my hand, my... my hand became red from his blood. He was not on a stage to say a single word. I shouted for help, but nobody came outside. They all were looking from their window. They were scared too. My mother came but she fainted after seeing so much blood. I was a teenage boy by that time. I don't know what to do. My father took his last breath in my hand. Manoj eyes were wet after saying this. He controlled his emotions.

Mr. Chaitanya: Oh, so sad. But from that day, my connections got bigger. But the true story was, I did not kill your father. Mr. Luthra did. I was just doing business for him. If I got jail, then his business would be ruined.

Manoj: I will kill Mr. Luthra too. You both were partners, right? Then how come I left him alone?

Manoj took his gun from behind his pocked and pointed to Mr. Chaitanya's head. But Mr. Chaitanya slapped his hand and threw the gun away. They both had a major fight. Mr. Chaitanya grabbed his head and hit the mirror, and he got injured. Mr. Chaitanya started laughing at him.

Mr. Chaitanya: You are not like your father Manoj. I am already injured and can still fight with you. You don't deserve to be a police Inspector. Look at me, I am 55 years old, and you are only thirty-two or thirty-three. Come on, get up and fight like your father.

Anaya shouted from the corner.

Anaya: Manoj, you can't beat him. He took steroids, which is why he became so powerful.

Mr. Chaitanya went at Anaya, grabbed his head, and hit the closet.

Mr. Chaitanya: I don't want to hear any commentary. So, where are we? Yes, come on. Fight.

Manoj tried to stand up but because of hit on head, he become unconscious. He had blurry vision. Mr. Chaitanya punched him again and he fell on the ground.

Mr. Chaitanya: You lost Manoj Shekhar Khare. Just like your father. I am not interested in fighting with you more. Let us end this.

He took a gun and pointed at Manoj head. Manoj slapped his hand and threw it towards Anaya. Mr. Chaitanya punched him in the face. Anaya woke up

unconsciously and found a gun near to her. She held the gun, pointed at Mr. Chaitanya, and shouted.
Anaya: Rajappa Chaitanya.
As soon as Mr. Chaitanya turned back, Anaya shot him in the left hand. Mr. Chaitanya fell on the ground and Anaya started crying. The music was so loud that gunshots could not be heard. Manoj got up and started punching Mr. Chaitanya. He got weak. Manoj punched him and he fell on the ground. He sat on Mr. Chaitanya and repetitively punched him.
Manoj: You should not kill my father. You should not. You will die.
Manoj grabbed the gun and shot his right hand. Mr. Chaitanya cried out in pain. Manoj kept gun aside and punched him again on face.
Manoj: You will get what you deserve.
Manoj stopped for a while. Mr. Chaitanya's face was so bloody. He was facing between life and death. He saw Manoj and tried to say something.
Manoj: What? You want me to stop here? Are you begging for your life? Afraid of being death?
Manoj started punching him again. After a few more punches, he grabbed a gun and pointed to his forehead.
Manoj: This is for my father.
Manoj shot Mr. Chaitanya. Manoj's father's justice has been served. After a few seconds, Manoj became unconscious. Anaya went at him.
Anaya: Manoj, come on. We must leave from here.
Manoj manages to wake up and stood up with the help of Anaya. They see Raja is still alive. Manoj went at her and chocked him to death.

**

Manoj and Anaya both tried to sneak out the window. The Villa was away from the city and the property was so big that no one can hear or know what is happening to another Villa. After walking for a while, Santosh was ready with a car. They both entered the car and Santosh took them to hospital. Anaya took his head and put it in her lap. She was scared after seeing so much blood loss. She started crying.

Anaya: Manoj don't close your eyes. Talk to me continuously. We are on our way to the hospital. Wake up. Santosh, please drive fast.

Manoj: Ana... Anaya.

Anaya: Yes, Manoj. Don't close your eyes.

Manoj: Th... Thank you. Thank you for your support. I... It is like, you gave taken a huge burden took off my shoulder. I took my father's revenge. He... He will be so proud of me. I want to meet him.

Manoj held her hand for a while. But he fainted. Anaya got scared and shouted.

Anaya: Manoj. No, no. Wake up. Santosh, please drive fast. Wake up Manoj please.

**

They arrived at the hospital. Santosh opened the door and male nurse came with stretcher. They took him quickly to the operating theatre where the doctor started examining him. A nurse came to Anaya and supported him by giving him water. She later asked Santosh about it and asked the police to complain.

Santosh: This is some personal matter. I request you to please keep it a secret.

A nurse understood and left them without saying anything. The doctor came from operation theatre after a few hours.

Doctor: Don't worry. He is out of danger. There has been heavy blood loss due to pieces of glass entering the head. He will remain unconscious for some time. Santosh sir, can I talk to you for a moment?

Santosh went with the doctor to his cabin.

Doctor: I know you are a savior, and you know the rules. What exactly happened?

Santosh: It is a big story, doctor. And I can't even explain in short. I just want you to keep it a secret and not mention it at any place or to anyone.

Doctor: I understand. Although Manoj is a great person. I will not let anyone know about it. Maybe he won't recognize me, but he saved my daughter getting kidnapped years ago. Just give him these medicines when he wakes up. We shifted him to the ICU special room. A nurse will be there all the time. He got beaten badly and his hands broke. It will take time, but he will rejoin in a few months.

The doctor gave Santosh a list of medicines for Manoj.

Santosh: When will we meet Manoj sir?

Doctor: You can meet him, but he is not in a state to listen to anything. He will examine him for forty-eight hours.

Santosh left from there. Anaya asked Santosh what the doctor said.

Santosh: He is unconscious only. The doctor will examine him for 48 hours. A nurse will always be there to help. Come, I will drop you at your home.

Anaya: No, it is okay. I will stay here with him. Can I meet him?

Santosh: Ma'am, he is not in the phase to hear you. What will you do?

Anaya: I don't know. I just want to stay with him. He has nobody to take care of him.

Santosh: He does not have a family, but I am always there for him. He always treated me as a younger brother. Although, I am older than him. You go and rest at home. I will take care of him.

Santosh tries to convince Anaya, but she did not want left Manoj.

**

Anaya went into ICU and stood beside him. She wanted to stay with him till he regained consciousness. It was midnight, Anaya was also tired. She took a stool and sat on it. Later, she felt asleep besides Manoj. In a few hours, Manoj hand shook. He was awake and saw Anaya asleep beside him. He tried to move his body a little bit and Anaya woke up.

Anaya: Manoj, are you okay? Nurse, please call the doctor.

Manoj: My mind feels heavy. Why are you here? You should go home and rest.

Anaya: You saved me last night. How can I leave you like this? Thank you.

Manoj: I want to Thank you for saving my life. To help me to take revenge. Still Mr. Luthra left to kill but I will catch him too. He was also involved in this.

Doctor: Okay, Manoj. Anaya, can I please? How do you feel?

4.24 - A Date & A Time

Manoj: My mind feels heavy, stitches you give hurts a little bit and I am so hungry.

Anaya: I bring fruits and inform Santosh about it too.

Anaya brought fruits after a while. Santosh came too to meet Manoj.

Santosh: How do you feel today sir?

Manoj: Good, very good. What have you told them about me?

Santosh: Nothing much. You had an accident, and you need rest for a few months.

Manoj: Few months? No. Start working on Mr. Luthra's file. He is also a culprit in this.

Anaya: Relax, Manoj. Everything has its time. The thing will be going to happen whether you want it or not. Take a break and start your work after a few weeks only. Till then, Santosh will ready the file for you.

**

Anaya got a call from Shekhar. She left outside to attend.

Anaya: Yes, Shekhar. What happened?

Shekhar: We must go to the villa where Mr. Chaitanya was murdered.

Anaya looked inside the room. Santosh and Manoj both were smiling and laughing.

Anaya: You know what? I can't come to work. Tell them I am on leave for a few weeks. Some personal work.

Anaya hung up the call joined with Manoj and Santosh. In the evening, Santosh bought dinner for all three.

Manoj: What have you got?

Santosh: It is just Sabu dana Khichadi. You are ill and the doctor told us not to give anything heavy.
Anaya: What for us? Sabu dana Khichadi?
Santosh: No. We will eat Chicken Biryani. Manoj sirs must look at us while eating. He feels jealous and sad.
Manoj: Come on. Don't do this to me. I also want Biryani. You guys eat Chicken and what I eat! Khichadi?
Santosh: You wanted to go and catch Mr. Chaitanya. You got hurt and the doctor asked for bed rest, it is your fault. Why should we bear it? You must eat Khichadi, and we will eat Biryani. Take this packet Anaya.
Santosh passed the food packet to Anaya, and she was happy, and Manoj got upset. When Anaya opened it, it was Khichadi too.
Anaya: What? It is also Sabu dana Khichadi.
Santosh: I know. Sir also likes Biryani very much. Manoj sirs eat khichdi, and we eat biryani Infront of him, it won't feel good. We will also give company to him. People come first to participate in the happiness of others, but those who are with us even in sorrow are our own.
Anaya turned on the television for the news.
Reporter: Chennai's mafia Mr. Rajappa Chaitanya and his so-called right-hand Raja shot dead in villa. His gang has been arrested from there. Police found minor girls from there whom Mr. Chaitanya was going to sell to in foreign countries. We wanted to thank whoever gave the information about it to the police as well as news reporters. Also, police found various types of

drugs and injections in box which maybe they are going to supply. And yes, it is also proven that the drug supplier in the whole North region was Mr. Rajappa Chaitanya. We…

Manoj snatches remote from Anaya's hand and turns it off.

Anaya: Isn't it great? We saved so many lives. Right, Manoj? What do you think?

Manoj: Mr. Bose, Mr. Khanna, Mr. Jain, Mr. Sisodia, and now Mr. Chaitanya. You see what is common between them? They all were working under or with Mr. Luthra. Murderer killed only those people who were close to Mr. Luthra. Where is Mr. Luthra?

Santosh: Come on, sir. We solved the biggest problem of the state and you still thinking about him? He ran away.

Manoj: No, Santosh. You don't know his story. He is not a coward. He is a lion, and surely will show his true power.

*****

Chapter 4

You realized you are on the wrong path. You are changing it. Good. But make sure you are heading in the right direction.

4.24 - A Date & A Time

New Delhi. 9th October 2016

Four months have been passed and no major case has been registered in any police station. Chain snatching, vehicle thief and only small cases have been registered. Also, police were only trying to close an old case. Everything was going great but who knew that a storm was about to come. A storm in which everyone will drown. Not only single city, but whole north region.

Mr. Luthra was so upset and angry related to his businesses. In these last few months, he dropped from the top 10 Asia's richest person to top 50. In these few months, he lost his money, customers, power, and reputation from industry. He wanted all the things back that he lost at any cost.

Mr. Luthra was in his Delhi hotel office sitting on a chair. He was holding a fork in right hand eating fruit bowl and fruit juice on left hand. His personal assistant named Riya was standing Infront of him.

Mr. Luthra: How much in last quarter?

Riya: 5.47% less.

Mr. Luthra: Where?

Riya: Major is in hotels. Heard that our guests were not receiving packets, so they left from there.

Mr. Luthra: I know the reason. Have you contacted other dealers? What have they said?

Riya: They were afraid of doing it, sir. They were afraid of doing with you and how Mr. Chaitanya died. May I know what is in the packets and why they are all afraid of you? I mean, you are very calm…

Mr. Luthra: Call Mr. Srinivasan for a meeting.

4.24 - A Date & A Time

Riya: Okay, sir.

Riya left from there. As soon as the door closed, he left his demon out. He stood from his chair and threw a glass on mirror. Because of the sound, Riya entered the room.

Riya: What happened, sir? Are you okay?

Mr. Luthra: Yes, I am. Can you please call someone and clear this? Broken glass brings bad luck in the house.

Mr. Luthra had two different personalities. One was business mind, calm, does not feel anger and cares for everyone. Second was mafia, rapist, manufacturing and supplying of illegal drugs, anger, and sometimes a killer. He shows his First personality for legal business and second for illegal business. Riya tried to call Mr. Srinivasan's secretary for a meeting. She also sends an email regarding this, but he was not ready to meet with the mafia. Mr. Srinivasan knows Mr. Luthra's businesses.

The very next day, Mr. Luthra asked Riya about it.

Mr. Luthra: Anything from Mr. Srinivasan?

Riya: I am trying but he did not want to meet you.

Mr. Luthra: Okay. Do you know where he is now?

Riya: He is in Chennai for the next two days and then he left for London for a meeting. It is inside information got from someone close.

Mr. Luthra: Arrange a plane for me please to go to Chennai. I will fly tonight and will meet him directly.

Riya: Okay, sir.

Riya left from there. Mr. Luthra opened Mr. Srinivasan's Wikipedia. He wanted to know past and present to somehow choke him. He is the only one who can help to save his business and power. But Mr. Luthra knows that Mr. Srinivasan will not easily help in this matter.

**

The other side, Forensic team was trying to find the killer of Mr. Chaitanya. It was still a mystery. It was handled by another team of forensic.

Aditya: It has been more than Four months now and we got nothing. What will I tell the court? We got so much evidence but not matching with anyone. How? I also asked Sanjay if they got anything, but he never gave the right answer to me. What should I do!

***

Aditya was a short-tempered person in the whole department. Most of the cases he solved in less than two months. He was addicted to drink. At Mr. Chaitanya's murder site, he got fingerprints, skin, blood, and hair samples. He tried to match everyone's which was present and got caught but did not match anyone. He got frustrated and broke the flask in the lab.

***

Dhairya: Sir, control. Please sit here. Don't worry, we will find them soon. Drink water. Calm down. We already asked to get footage of the road, we are too close to catch them.

***

Dhairya was the only one who could handle him. Both were college friends, and he worked as an assistant of Aditya.

***

Aditya: Do one think. There is whiskey in my droor. Also, bring the ice cubes to the fridge.

Dhairya brought whiskey and Aditya drunk 60ML in one go.

Dhairya: Sir, what are you doing? Your level will fail.

Aditya: Stop it. I know what I am doing and how to handle it. Don't be shy, you can drink too.

Aditya made a glass for him and added two ice cubes. They both started drinking and forget about the work.

Aditya: My work, my reputation was screwed because of that Anaya. Because of her, management is not giving me cases like before. Who the hell his she to complaint about my drinking problem. Yes, I drink, but work will be done as I committed. But no. Because of her. I will take revenge.

**

After four months, Manoj joined again after fitness and medical test to rejoin the department. People were unaware what he had accepted Santosh. When he entered, everybody stood up and saluted and gave him respect. Santosh had a smile on his face and saluted for what he had done. Manoj directly went to his cabin.

Santosh: Good to see you on duty, Manoj Khare sir.

Manoj: Good to see you too and my cabin, desk, smell. Feel like ready to fight again.

Santosh: How is your hand, sir?

Manoj: It feels good. It can't move easily now but hope it will. Somehow, I managed to clear the fitness test to rejoin and let us see what we have. Bring the file of pending cases.

Santosh: We don't do anything right now sir. All the major cases were closed, and minor cases is handling the team like chain snatching and all.

Manoj: Great to hear that. What about Mr. Luthra? Have…

Santosh: It is ready, but we have other things to do. Remember four months ago, we ran from Mr. Chaitanya's villa and took Highway to reach hospital?

Manoj: I don't because I was unconscious. What about it?

Santosh: Aditya and Dhairya are handling the forensic part, and they asked Haresh to get CCTV recordings of whoever went from that road. There are high chances we will get caught.

Manoj: Haresh? That Gujarati, right? I know him well. I will handle him and don't worry about it. Is he handling this case?

Santosh: Yes, he is. How will you handle it?

Manoj: Don't worry about it. Is there anything else?

Santosh: Not now. Hopefully, we will not because I was in the front seat who is driving the car. First, they will catch me.

Manoj: Don't worry, Santosh. No one will hurt you until I am here.

Manoj called Haresh to meet. He offered to come to his police station.

**

In a few hours, Haresh came to meet Manoj.

Haresh: Manoj, how are you? I heard that you met with an accident. Is everything okay?

Manoj: I am good. I wanted to discuss that accident with you and need your help. The thing is…
Haresh: What happened Manoj? Is there any problem?
Manoj: I want to discuss Mr. Chaitanya's murder. It was done by me.
Haresh: What? By legally or?
Haresh was shocked after hearing this. Manoj explained him whole back story of it. And asked him to delete the footage of that night.
Haresh: I am so sorry Manoj, but you are late. I already gave the footage to Sanjay sir. You know how cruel he is. It has been a few months since I gave it to him. If you said earlier on the phone, then I will not.
Manoj: It is okay, Haresh. I will take care of it.
Manoj behaved like it is a normal thing, but he is worried about Santosh.

***

Sanjay was an ex-army Inspector. He was brutally injured in a fight and was on bed rest for more than three years. He tried to re-join the army, but the government disagreed. Sanjay was so enthusiastic that he wanted to serve the country at any cost. So, he went to parliament, and they deputed him as a Police Inspector at Delhi's police station. He was too crucial for criminals as he was an ex-army Inspector. He felt nothing for the criminal until he was found not guilty.

***

Manoj started to get curious for Santosh and Anaya. Suddenly, Sanjay entered his Police Station. He held an envelope and stick in his hand and two police constables walking behind him. Everybody stood up and saluted him. Not with respect but fear. He entered in Manoj's cabin. Manoj stood up from his chair and salute.

Manoj: Jai hind.

Sanjay: Relax. Jai hind Mr. Manoj Khare. How are you doing?

Manoj: I am doing good sir. How are you?

Sanjay: Not good. I heard that you met with an accident. Is it true?

Manoj started sweating.

Manoj: Yes, sir. I was on bed rest for a few months.

Sanjay: Whatever. Where is Santosh? We are here to arrest him. Don't waste my time and call him.

Manoj: Santosh? Arrest? What happened?

Sanjay: Why are scared and shocked? Do you know what he did?

Manoj: No, I know nothing. Maybe he is outside.

Santosh arrived with food in his hand. He does not know what was happening in that room. He looked at Manoj and said quietly 'I am sorry.' Sanjay hit his stick to Santosh's stomach so hard that he fell on the ground.

Manoj: Hey, what are you doing? You can't hit my man like that. You don't have any right to do this.

Sanjay throws that envelope to Manoj's desk. See that and then say. He was present that day when Mr. Chaitanya got murdered. We found him driving a car from that. May I know Santosh what were you doing?

Manoj: You can't hit a person from just a clip. He was there does not prove that he killed Mr. Chaitanya. Maybe he was doing something personal.

Sanjay: Oh, personal. Santosh, are you married? If yes, then you should do in your room and not in someone's private party and killed them.

Sanjay kicked Santosh. He saw Manoj's eyes and felt something weird.

Sanjay: I received this footage few months back Manoj. But I wanted to show you that your man is a culprit. You were feeding a snake.

Sanjay again tried to kick Santosh, but Manoj could not control himself and pushed Sanjay from him and shouted.

Manoj: He did not kill him, I killed him. I was the one who shot his head.

Sanjay: I knew it. I knew something was wrong. What a friendship my love. He did not say anything to save you, and you said everything to save him. Great. Boys handcuff him and take both to our police station.

Manoj: Let Santosh go. I committed a crime, and I accepted.

Sanjay: As per me, this is not how law works. I will teach you at my station.

Sanjay's team handcuffed both. Everyone in the police station as well as out of station to them. Sanjay called the media and informed them to come to the police station. They all arrived, and the media waited to telecast the news to their channel. They all gathered around them and started asking questions.

Reporter: Sir, sir. Is it true that Police Inspector Manoj is behind the murder of Mr. Chaitanya?

Sanjay: Criminal is not guilty until they found. We have some evidence, and we only wanted to match it.

Reporter: If he is not guilty then why do you handcuff them?
Sanjay: Police can handcuff anyone so that they will not run from it and bring them to the police station if they have doubt for an interrogation. I don't think you learned something about how the police work. Now, let us do our work so that the murderer gets caught. Come on, move.

**

Sanjay took them all to the interrogation room. His team made them sit on a chair beside each other and tied their hands and feet with a rope.
Manoj: Let Santosh go, Sanjay.
Sanjay: Sir. Call me Sanjay sir. Here in this room, you are a criminal, and I am an Inspector. We are not friends. Start with Santosh. Tell me, what happened that night?
Santosh was scared. He sweated a lot. He looked at Manoj for a second.
Sanjay: I asked you Santosh. Don't make me do this.
Santosh: Mr. Chaitanya was a criminal. It is good if he died, then why all of this?
Sanjay: He is a criminal, we all agreed. But he was the government person of the South region. Did you know Manoj before killing him?
Manoj got shocked and scared. His body started getting cold, his throat started getting dry like a criminal.
Manoj: I… I did not know about it. When… When did it happen? I… I have… I have no idea Sanjay sir.

Sanjay: When you went to that villa. There was a party going on. Do you know what that is for?
Manoj: Drugs, girls supplying…
Sanjay: And entering the government of Mr. Chaitanya. He stood for MLA post from AKQ's party which relates to Mr. Luthra. There was Mr. Luthra who was also present in the party. Hope you knew about it. He ran from there so he would not get caught and nobody knew that he was present there. Because of Mr. Luthra's suggestion, Mr. Chaitanya's got a ticket for MLA. He asked Mr. Srinivasan too but he knew how Mr. Luthra was. If you did not know all of this and you killed him then you made a mistake.
Manoj and Santosh both were scared. They started sweating and their lips were dried.
Sanjay: Manoj, if I let you or Santosh go then he will surely be going to kill both of you. You fall his business, name, fame, money, power everything. I am here to protect you, not to kill you. I trust whatever your confession will be. Santosh, your footage of driving by that road, and Manoj, your blood and fingerprints on gun, floor and on Mr. Chaitanya's body is the proof that you killed him. I will try you both will get less punishments as you killed a mafia and not an MLA. He was about to stand up, that is why we can try to convenience court to him as a criminal. I am giving both of you some time to think and give a confession.
Sanjay left from there. Two constables untie them and leave the room too. Manoj and Santosh looked at each other.
Santosh: Anaya?

Manoj: Shush… He does not know about her. She did not do anything there. She helped me to kill him. We must confess the truth where Anaya's name will be not present. You only drove me to hospital and said the doctor's name, nothing else. I will say what I did there.

Santosh: But sir, you will get punished for good. Is there not any other option?

Manoj: No. Sanjay is an ex-army Inspector. He knows that our intention was not wrong. I saw truth in his eyes. He is with us and won't let anything wrong happen to us.

Suddenly, Sanjay entered the room with two constables.

Sanjay: So? Have you decided what to do?

Manoj moved his head in Yes. Sanjay asked one constable to note their confessions. First, Manoj confessed the crime where there is no mention of Anaya. Second, Santosh confessed that he took Manoj to hospital and doctor name.

Sanjay: Have you talked with the doctor about this? What if your both confessions got separated from each other?

Sanjay asked Manoj and he had no idea what to do. Sanjay called him and gave it to Manoj. Manoj explained to the doctor what to say in court.

Doctor: There was a girl too. Should I say her name too?

Manoj: No. It is not required. Just say what I say. After the discussion, he hung up.

Sanjay saw Manoj and felt weird again.

Sanjay: Is there anything else you both wanted to say? Is there anyone else with you?

Manoj looked in his eyes and nodded his head in No.

Manoj: I have a question, sir. If you want to help us, then why you call the News channel?

Sanjay: Sorry to say this but, you are so dumb, Manoj. If Mr. Luthra get to know that you killed Mr. Chaitanya, then he will try to kill you. With the help of News channels, I sent him a message that you are under my custody. And here my friend, you are safe. You have my full permission to research Mr. Chaitanya's business and how to catch Mr. Luthra on one condition. You can't leave this police station. You will get a bed, food, and all the files in the storeroom. If you want anything other than that, you can ask my constables.

Sanjay was about to leave but Manoj stopped him.

Manoj: How much time it will take to release us? Do you have any plans?

Sanjay: You must plan this. Not me. You will be going to either jail or dead. You both should thank me for helping you. As soon as you confess the judge that the man you killed was a criminal. You should gather evidence against him. I am leaving and both will stay with you.

Manoj: Can I make a call?

Sanjay: Anytime. There is a landline.

Sanjay left from there. Manoj and Santosh both transferred to storeroom where they had an old computer and lots of files.

On the other side, Mr. Luthra's assistant Riya was trying to contact and set a meeting with Mr. Srinivasan. But his assistant always replied that he is busy with something.

Riya: Sir, he is not responding. Can't we discuss with Mr. Gabrielle about business. He is the 12th richest person in the world. Although…

Mr. Luthra: No. I only want to meet Mr. Srinivasan. Do one thing, arrange a plane for me to Chennai. I will go there and meet him personally.

Riya: Okay, sir. Till midnight, we will leave for Chennai.

Mr. Luthra: Not you, Riya. I am going alone. I need nobody to come with me or follow me.

In the evening, Mr. Luthra left for the airport with the driver. He looked so calm and had no facial expression. But his heart was beating fast. He was scared and curious about his power. It was a three-hour long flight. For this time, he was only thinking how to convince Mr. Srinivasan.

When he arrived at the airport, one person was there to pick up Mr. Luthra. His name was Rafiq. They went to the car and Rafiq opened the front door for him.

***

A few months back, Rafiq was working for Mr. Chaitanya. Almost twenty years back, Mr. Luthra found Rafiq on the road begging when he was seventeen years old. That time Mr. Luthra does not have power so, that he asked Rafiq to sell drugs while begging. Also, he was deaf. So, no one even doubted him. When Mr. Luthra asked Mr. Chaitanya to work for him, he did not trust him and asked Rafiq to keep an eye on him. Rafiq was like a pet of Mr. Luthra. They both talk in sign language. If he says run, he will run. And if he says kill, he will kill; without even asking.

***

Mr. Luthra: What do you get?

Rafiq opened the front glove box. There was a gun and an envelope. He took an envelope and gave it to him.

Rafiq (In Sign Language): I looked at everything I could, but he does not have any weaknesses in business. He does not care about money. There is 0.0001% chance that any of his business will fall but if it happens, then he can build again in no time. He has only one weakness, his family. Here are the photos. He has only one child who is married and have a one granddaughter which is fifteen-year-old.

Mr. Luthra: Bring his son and daughter-in-law.

Rafiq (In Sign Language): What? Why can't we directly hit his granddaughter? He will surely give you what you want.

Mr. Luthra: He must give what I want at any cost. Just do as I say. I have other plans too. And you know where to bring them and what to do. I am so tired. Take to me the hotel and arrange some company for me.

**

Rafiq drove him to one of his hotels in Chennai. When they reached there, one of the guards opened the door for Mr. Luthra. He entered the hotel, and the manager came to welcome him.

Hotel Manager: Welcome sir. It has been a long time since you arrived here.

Mr. Luthra: Thank you so much. I know it has been a while. I came here for a very important meeting. Have you arranged all the amenities for me?

Hotel Manager: Yes, sir. I have already got a message from your secretary. I will take you to the room; the food will be delivered, and your special guests will be there too.

Hotel Manager took him to his room. He opened the door for Mr. Luthra.

Hotel Manager: Your luggage is already here. Call me for anything sir.

The Hotel Manager left from there. He went to the washroom to freshen up. After half an hour, ring bells of the room. He opened the door. There was a girl. He wore a golden dress, held a wallet and a ponytail. She was none other than Ms. India Yuvika Gautam.

***

Mr. Luthra saw Yuvika in a club in 2013. By that time, she was only twenty-three-years-old. She looked so beautiful, bold, and dancing on the floor that Mr. Luthra fell in love with her. Mr. Luthra offered her to be a model, and she accepted the offer. Reporters got the news about them it became the hottest news in media. Somehow, Mr. Luthra closed it with his power. They both denied dating each other on media conferences. Yuvika became Miss India 2015 only because of Mr. Luthra's recommendation.

***

Yuvika: Hello, Mr. Luthra. How are you? It has been a long time since we met.

Mr. Luthra looked at her from top to bottom. He grabbed her hand, pulled her into the room and closed the door.

Mr. Luthra: Has anybody seen you coming here?

Yuvika: Come on, darling. No one saw me. But I want to see you all day and all night.

Mr. Luthra smiled, grabbed her hand, pushed towards him, and hugged her tightly.

Mr. Luthra: I missed you too, my love. I missed you so much. Don't know how many months I have been waiting for this day. I want you so badly.

Yuvika: Then why don't you marry me?

Mr. Luthra fell silent for a second. He took a step and held her shoulder.

Yuvika: If you love me so much then why don't you accept Infront of society. I want to marry you.

Mr. Luthra: Darling, I am already married. I have a child. I love you too, but our love will be partial. This society won't accept our true love. Let us forget all the things, darling.

They started kissing each other. In the evening, Mr. Luthra was standing on the balcony and drinking a whiskey and cigar. Yuvika was lying on a bed. She woke up and went at Mr. Luthra.

Yuvika: What are you thinking?

Mr. Luthra: My Business…

Yuvika: Stop, darling. Why are you always thinking about it? Every time either business or power. You are still the number one for me. I told you that when you are with me, just stay with me. Business, money, and power are temporary things in life. True things are love and family.

Mr. Luthra: You know what, darling? Whatever you are and you have today is just because of business, money, and power. If I haven't done that, then you will be nothing today.

Yuvika was shocked after hearing this. She thought she hurt his feelings. Mr. Luthra put his hand on Yuvika's shoulder and kissed her forehead.

Mr. Luthra: Just thing, I lost all my business, power, and money. Do you still stay with me? You will also lose everything that you have.

Yuvika: Of… Of course, Dar… Darling. I love you.

Yuvika hugged her tightly. Mr. Luthra smiled a little.

Mr. Luthra: Go and get ready for the party, darling. I have a visitor too.

Yuvika: What will I do? I don't have any friends here. And we can't spend time together Infront of people.

Mr. Luthra: We will today. Give me some time and we both will have a romantic dinner together.

Yuvika got so happy and left to get ready. Mr. Luthra messaged Rafiq to be ready with the box. After a few minutes, Mr. Luthra left for the party in the hotel's club. Later, Yuvika also left the room. Yuvika was in the hotel, and everybody knows that people gathered and took a photo, videos, and autograph of her. Media was not allowed in the hotel, so she could freely move there. She was going to a club, but accidentally she bumped into Anaya.

***

4.24 - A Date & A Time

A few days back when Manoj and Santosh were in storeroom, Manoj calls Anaya for help.

Manoj: Hey, Anaya. Manoj here.

Anaya: Yes, what happened? You sound scared. Is everything alright?

Manoj: No. Santosh and I stuck somewhere, and we need your help. Remember Mr. Chaitanya's incident? He was the culprit, and we punished him. There is one more person there. Mr. Luthra. He was the main culprit behind all the rape, illegal drug supply, kidnapping and all. You must track him and gather information about it.

Anaya: Again? I am a forensic person. Not the detective or anything like that. Okay. I will try to track him and contact you.

Manoj: No, no. Don't call my number. I will call you twice a day.

***

Anaya: Oh, I am sorry. Are you okay?

Yuvika: Yes. Thank you.

Anaya left from there. Yuvika was a Miss India, and whenever people saw her, they started taking photos and autographs. But Anaya did not do anything which made her think about it. Later in the club, Anaya again bumped into Yuvika.

Anaya: Hey, it is you again. I am sorry.

Yuvika: No problem. Are you following me because I am Miss India? Are you a reporter or something?

Anaya: No, not at all. I know who you are, but it does not make me feel 'Yay, I met miss India' or anything. I am stressed about work, nothing else. I am sorry again.

Anaya started walking but Yuvika stopped her.
Yuvika: Hey, listen. Want to have a drink with me? I know you are stressed but I don't have any friends here. You sound a way different from the normal person.
Anaya: Sure, but is not it weird to have a drink with complete normal person and a miss India?
Yuvika: Come on. I am also a normal girl who is living, eating, and doing stuff like a normal person. I am not forcing you, but I am alone here, no media, no friends, which is why I asked for it.
Anaya: Okay. I am coming with you. But I will not drink alcohol as I am Muslim. Hi, I am Anaya Kadri.
Yuvika: Oh, Hi. I am Yuvika Gautam.
Anaya: You don't need to introduce yourself. Everyone knows about you.
Yuvika: I know but we first time, and I am going to drink alcohol whole night. When I get drunk, I will start crying, so I need you to support me.
Anaya: Don't worry. I will be there for you.
Anaya and Yuvika both went to the bar. Anaya ordered food for herself, and Yuvika ordered a bottle of alcohol. Anaya saw Mr. Luthra walking in a private party room and after a few minutes Mr. Srinivasan entered there. Anaya and Yuvika started talking about each other's life. Anaya introduced herself as a Lawyer and from Indore. Yuvika started talking about her journey of miss India. After a few rounds of alcohol, she started sharing feelings with Anaya.

4.24 - A Date & A Time

Yuvika: You know Ana. There is a person whom I love the most. But I can't live a life with him like a normal person.

Anaya: Why? Family issue?

Yuvika: No. Do I look like a person who could not convince parents? Look at me. I am Miss India 2015, a model, can cook good Indian food, and have money. But still, we can't either marry or stay with each other.

Anaya: Then what is your problem?

Anaya got bored hearing Yuvika's story. She did not have any interest in hearing it. She was there at the party because Mr. Luthra was there.

Yuvika: The problem is Luthra. He was between us. Because of him, we both can't freely hang out. His bodyguards always have an eye on me.

Anaya was stunned hearing this. She had no idea that Yuvika was Mr. Luthra's girlfriend. Yuvika made a strong drink and took a neat sip. She points to a person.

Yuvika: Look there. He is the one of Luthra's bodyguards who always keeps an eye on me.

Anaya: What? Mr. Luthra? The great businessman? But he has a wife and children. I think you are drunk, and you don't have any idea what you are saying. Please stop drinking.

Yuvika: You don't believe me? Wait. Where is my mobile? Look, look at this. Look at this girl sleeping with Luthra. Does her face not match mine? You still don't believe me? I have other proof too. Look at our photos. This one when we were at dinner, and in a room. Oh, our make-out video. Do you want to see it?

Anaya: No. What? I believe you. Okay. Please stop. And stop drinking.

Yuvika: Because of him, my boyfriend and I can't hang out freely.

Anaya: If you are not interested in Mr. Luthra, then why can't you leave him? He has a family, and you are the extra. You should back out.

Yuvika: I can't. He made me Miss India. He made me who I am today. Whatever I have today is his. If I leave him, then he will end my career, my future, and kill every person I have. I was a kid when he offered me the chance to become a model. At that time, I did not know what to do. He shows me a light, a path which can take me to heaven. Who knows that the path will went to hell. I must fake smile whenever he is around me.

Anaya was so shocked that she could not say anything. Yuvika again made a strong drink. Anaya tried to stop her, but she resisted and drank it. Yuvika was so drunk and did not have any idea what she was saying and to whom.

Yuvika: His every touch on my body feels like… I always wanted to kill him. But I could not. I wish I had a chance to slap at least once.

Yuvika started vomiting. Anaya wanted to sit there and want to know what was going on inside Mr. Luthra's party room. Anaya grabbed her hand, put it on shoulder, and took her to the washroom. Yuvika vomited.

Anaya: Okay, alright. I told you not to drink so much. How you guys like this thing.

Yuvika: Thank you, Ana. Thanks for…
Yuvika again puke.
Anaya: No need to say anything. You need sleep. What is your room number?
Yuvika: Penthouse. Can we have a shot of vodka, please?
Anaya: No. No more alcohol.
Anaya took her to the room. She put her on bed.
Yuvika: Thank you, Ana. Tomorrow morning, I will plan to kill Luthra. I want you to support me in it.
Yuvika slept after saying this, and Anaya left the room. On the other side Mr. Luthra and Mr. Srinivasan made a deal for the upcoming business. Not friendly, but forcefully. When Mr. Srinivasan entered the party room, Mr. Luthra had two dancers on both sides, whiskey in one hand, and cigar in other.
Mr. Luthra: Hello, my old friend. I was waiting for you.
Mr. Srinivasan: You? I came here to meet Mr. Yokohama.
Mr. Luthra: You were not responding to my secretary's mail or call, which is why I came here to visit like this. Please, take a sit.
Mr. Srinivasan: I don't want to talk with you. Because of you, so many people killed, murdered, and suicide. You were the reason my friend Chintu died. I don't want to talk with you about anything.
Mr. Srinivasan was about to leave but Mr. Luthra's bodyguard stopped him by blocking his way.
Mr. Luthra: I am sorry Mr. Srinivasan. You came here by your own choice, but you will leave when I say. You

know what else I can do, right? Now, take a seat and have a drink.

Mr. Srinivasan does not have any other option. He sits Infront of him.

Mr. Srinivasan: What do you want?

Mr. Luthra: You were the only one who was closest to Mr. Chaitanya, right? Tell me his all-business details. His supplying business, his people, and all the details that will make me rich and give me my power back.

Mr. Srinivasan: I know nothing about it. He was my friend but he neither told me, nor I asked about his business. I never wanted him to do it.

Mr. Luthra: Shush… Please call Rafiq.

Bodyguard called Rafiq. He took out his mobile and played an audio where Mr. Srinivasan and Mr. Chaitanya were discussing business back on 12th November 2016.

***

12th November 2016, Mr. Srinivasan visited Mr. Chaitanya's house. That day, Mr. Luthra offered him to supply drugs in North region.

Mr. Srinivasan: Hey, Chintu. I told you not to do this again.

Mr. Chaitanya: Not again. Come and sit here. I want to discuss all the details of this business with you.

Mr. Srinivasan: No. I don't want to hear this nonsense. I don't want to do business of this thing, then what will I do of taking this nonsense knowledge?

Mr. Chaitanya: Because one day someone will kill me, and the mastermind will do anything to know about the business. He will kill my entire family to know from where the money come from, who is my dealer. You are the only one who can save my family. Please.

Mr. Srinivasan: Chintu, if I knew anything about it, then he will also kill my family too.

Mr. Chaitanya: If not, then too. Because you are the only one who is closest to me.

Mr. Srinivasan: Who is he? What is his name?

Mr. Chaitanya: Kuldeep Singh Luthra. The businessman, and mastermind behind illegal businesses in India. He has fake medicine manufacturing companies, drug supplying, minor girl rape and supply them to foreign countries, and more. Many officers tried to catch him, but… They all got killed. I only want you to know what I am doing, how and with whom. If he asks or tortures you, you can say something to save yourself.

***

Mr. Srinivasan got scared. He knew that this time would come. He did not want to listen to Mr. Chaitanya's businesses, but he told him to save him.

Mr. Luthra: So, Mr. Srinivasan. Now, you know that I know. Please tell me everything about it.

Mr. Srinivasan: No. I will not tell you anything. You will be going to destroy the whole world. You already have money and power; then why do you waste other's life? You have hotels, bars, clubs, companies, and more. You should thank God what you have. Stop ruining people's life by giving them drugs.

Mr. Luthra: Krishan Indra Srinivasan. You have God's name in your whole name. But you are not a God. Do you want to meet them?

Mr. Luthra stood up and showed him his mobile phone. It was a video call with someone where his whole family was captured by Mr. Luthra's one of the killers. His wife, son, and daughter-in-law were tied up on a chair at the edge of seaport. Mr. Srinivasan got scared while seeing this. He shouted, pushed Mr. Luthra.

Mr. Srinivasan: Hey, you. No. Where are they? Where is my family? You can't do this. I will kill you.

Mr. Srinivasan took a whiskey bottle and tried to hit Mr. Luthra. His bodyguards grabbed the bottle and punched him in the face. He fell on the ground. He felt breathless.

Mr. Luthra: No, no. Don't hit him. He is our guest.

Mr. Srinivasan: Leave my family. They have nothing to do with it.

Mr. Srinivasan took his mobile phone and tried to call the police. Mr. Luthra took his phone too.

Mr. Luthra: Come on, Sri. I am not asking for money, or anything. Just give me information and I will let you and your family go.

Mr. Srinivasan: No.

Mr. Luthra: Push.

On video call, a person came and pushed his son into a sea.

Mr. Srinivasan: No. No. My son.

Mr. Srinivasan started crying.

Mr. Srinivasan: Luthra. Please. Let them go.

Mr. Luthra: Push.

On video call, the same person came again and pushed his daughter-in-law to sea.

Mr. Luthra: You know, I don't waste time. You have two options. Either you give me information and I let your wife live or I will kill your wife as well as you. Don't worry about me. I will ask someone else about Chintu's business.

Mr. Srinivasan: No. Stop, please. I will tell you everything. Please let her go.

Mr. Luthra sat. Mr. Srinivasan was on the floor. He shared every detail that he knew with contact details. After a few minutes, he stood up.

Mr. Srinivasan: I told you everything. Please let me and wife go. Please give me my son and daughter-in-law back.

Mr. Luthra: Okay. I trust you. Your family will be sent to your home safely. Your wife, son, and daughter-in-law.

Mr. Srinivasan was shocked. Mr. Luthra showed him a video call where his son and daughter-in-law were on a boat.

Mr. Luthra: They all are safe. I am not a bad person for a good person, Mr. Srinivasan. You are a very good person and doing great things for the world. Once, you were an ideal for me. But when I learned that it took you more than forty-years to earn fame, name, and money. I can't wait this long. You can go home. Your family will be sent home safely. No one will ever touch you again. You have my words and my security.

Mr. Srinivasan: I don't want anything from you. You will be going to die. You will not get death easily. Whatever deeds you have done in the past, will be paid. All the blood will flow from your body. You will be

struggling between life and death. You will beg for your life, but the God will let you suffer the pain you gave to others.
Mr. Luthra: Throw him out, boys.
Mr. Luthra's bodyguards grabbed Mr. Srinivasan and threw him out of the party room. Unfortunately, Anaya was entering that room as a waiter with food on plate. One of the bodyguards took it and asked her to leave.
Rafiq (Sign Language): What now?
Mr. Luthra: I am going into my room. We will leave tomorrow for Delhi. Till then, contact everyone and call for a meeting. Let our business grow with money and power.
Mr. Luthra left for this room. He saw Yuvika sleeping.
Mr. Luthra: Darling. I don't think I want you anymore. I got another option. From tomorrow, live your life as you wanted. Like every other woman lives with family, and your boyfriend. I want to see how far you can go without me.
Anaya got a call from Manoj. She informed about Yuvika and Mr. Luthra's affair.
Manoj: Oh. Stay in touch with her and try to get all the details she can give about him. We found news and closed FIRs about Mr. Luthra. He had done the worst things in the past. Drugs, rape, murder, lots of things. This time, no one could save him.
The very next day, Yuvika woke up in the morning and saw Mr. Luthra was sleeping on a couch. Her head felt heavy. She went to him. She slowly moved her hand on Mr. Luthra's head. Mr. Luthra awake.
Yuvika: Darling, why are you sleeping here?

Mr. Luthra: Because you took the whole bed. How are you doing, darling? How was your last night?
Yuvika: I feel hangover, so maybe great. I met a girl, and she helped me after getting drunk. Oh, my head feels heavy.
Mr. Luthra stood up and made a drink for her.
Mr. Luthra: Here, take it.
Yuvika drank it and went to the washroom. When she came, Mr. Luthra was not in the room. She thought he went somewhere and got busy on his mobile. She ordered breakfast for herself too. But, after a few more hours when he did not come back, she felt something weird. She tried to call him but did not pick up the phone. She tried to message him and call him till evening but got no response. Later, she got a call from Mr. Luthra's assistant Riya.
Riya: Hello. Am I speaking with Ms. Yuvika Gautam?
Yuvika: Yes, who is this?
Riya: This is Riya, Mr. Luthra's assistant. He told me to drop a message to you that he will not continue his bond with you. We found other models for advertising.
Yuvika: Bond? What are you? Where is he? Can I have a word with him?
Riya: I am sorry ma'am, but he is too busy in meetings. That is why he asked me to inform you about it. I hope you have a great future in your career. Thank you and have a good day.
Riya hung up the call. Yuvika did not have any idea what happened. After a few minutes she got a voice message from Mr. Luthra.

Mr. Luthra (Voice message): I know you are upset. I have a family. A wife and a child. You wanted a family too, which I can't give. Don't worry, your boyfriend will give you what you are seeking for. He is the right one for you. Although, you wanted to kill me, right? I gave you everything you wanted. Love, money, fame. I made you a model. Still, you betrayed me, darling. I called you moon, right? I said you will shine like a moon and will shine like a moonlight. But you forget that light is not own by moon. Moon shines because of sun, and I was your sun. I found out about this long ago, but I don't want to accept fate. When you came into my life, I lost my path. But, from now on you will walk alone. I am not going to meet you ever or kill you. I would love to see how far you will go without me.

Yuvika was stunned and fell on the ground after seeing this. She thought Mr. Luthra did not know about her other relationship. She knew that if he found out about her, he would end her future, and he had done. After a few minutes, Yuvika got a mail from the manager.

Manager (Mail): Dear Yuvika, we would like to inform you that we heard so many rumors about you which made our company's impressions down. Our head has decided to end the bond with you, and we will not be supporting or sponsoring you anymore. We hope you have a great future ahead.

Yuvika read this and started shouting and crying, she got another mail from brands that she signed to work with them. They all backout to work with her. Mr. Luthra ended her career as she expected. She does not know what to do or where to go. She got a call from Mumbai Police station.

Police: Is this Yuvika Gautam?

Yuvika: Yes, who is this?

Police: We found a guy named Rohit dead in river. We found his mobile phone on a sea link and your contact number saved as an emergency phone number. How do you know him?

Yuvika again shocked. She could not stand still and cried.

Police: Hello? Ma'am, are you alright?

Yuvika: He... He was... My love. He was my boyfriend. He does not have mother and father.

Police: We are sorry about it. Can you please...

Yuvika: I am in Chennai, and I'll be there in few hours.

She packed her bags to leave Mumbai. Accidentally, Anaya bumped into her again in the corridor.

Anaya: Hey, Yuvika. Are you alright?

Yuvika saw her and started crying. She hugged Anaya.

Anaya: Hey, what happened? Stop crying. Come to my room.

Anaya took her to my room which is on 10th floor. She offered her a glass of water and asked her about the situation.

Anaya: What happened? Why are you crying?

Yuvika: He had done what he wanted to. He killed my boyfriend. He used his power and end my career too. I can't do anything.

Anaya: Shush. It is okay. Please stop crying.

Yuvika: I am going to kill myself. Before he kills me, I'll will die. I want to end this.

Anaya got panicked. Yuvika stood up and tried to jump from the 10th floor of the Hotel. Anaya tried to stop her from suicide.

Anaya: No, Yuvika. Please stop.

Yuvika: Just let me go. He will kill me like he kills Rohit. I don't want to die from his hand.

Anaya grabbed her waist and slammed on bed. Somehow, she opened a bag on sniffed her a chloroform.

Anaya: It is okay. Stop. You don't have to do this. Relax. Be calm.

Due to chloroform, she fell asleep. Anaya took a rest for a minute, and then she got a call from Manoj.

Manoj: Hey, how are you? What is happening there?

Anaya: Horrible. I don't know how I can say this. I don't know from where to start.

Manoj: What happened?

Anaya told Manoj the whole story of Mr. Luthra and Yuvika. Manoj: Oh, God. I will handle here but please take care of Yuvika. She can be the strongest witness in the court. I will try to find about affair news.

Anaya: I was better in the Lab. I don't want to do this. I can't see people dying, killing each other Infront my eyes anymore.

Anaya started crying a little bit.

Manoj: Hey, Anaya. You are the one of the strongest persons I ever know. I will help you out from this mess. I am sorry because you are in the mess because of me. You just stay there and take care of Yuvika, and we will handle here.

4.24 - A Date & A Time

Anaya hung up the call without saying anything. She lied on bed besides Yuvika and watching ceiling. In the evening, Yuvika woke up and seeing Anaya besides her. She started crying again.

Yuvika: Ana. Please help me. I don't know what to do now.

Anaya continued looking to ceiling.

Anaya: Do you have family?

Yuvika: Yes.

Anaya: Are they happy with your success? Do they ask money from you?

Yuvika: There are happy with whatever I am doing. They never asked but I always send them for house and for a trip. They feel so proud. They can't see me cry. When I was a kid, I wanted a princess doll set, but my mother won't agree to buy because we didn't have that much money. I was a kid that time and didn't know or care about it so, I started crying and in a few hours my father bought it for me.

Anaya: Your father loves you so much. They sacrifice their priorities to fulfill yours. They wanted you to keep smile, keep live in the moment. You don't have money, fame, power but you started from zero. You are now there too. Your career is over but not your life.

Yuvika: But he killed my boyfriend, my love.

Anaya: He was your second love, or third. You loved him so much that you can't live without him. But doesn't your father love you too? Your first love is your family, second one is your career, and third one is your boyfriend. Last two is not with you but you have the most powerful thing in the world. Just think how they react when they see your body lying on mortuary. Think that about their face, that smile when they see your dead body. You are not even thirty. You still have a beautiful fifty or seventy years left in which you can earn again.

Yuvika: Ana. I…

Anaya: I can't help you with your future or your love, but I believe you can do anything you want. Don't worry about anything and keep going in life. Just remember the famous line; 'Whatever happens, happens for a reason.'

Yuvika sat and hugged her tightly. Yuvika cries continuously.

Yuvika: I am sorry, Ana. I got panicked.

Anaya: Shush. Don't cry. You don't have to say sorry to me. Say sorry to yourself that you lost control on yourself. You can start from your zero again. You will have either same life as before or better than before.

Yuvika: I am going home, and I will start from zero. I will not get back my foot. I will do something in life. I had a hand of Mr. Luthra when I was a model but now, there will be only one person who depends on myself, and it will be only me. There will be only one who can either make the path to the sky or destroy will be only me. I will do something. Thanks, Ana.

The other side, Mr. Luthra started contacting all the suppliers, dealers, and kidnappers who Mr. Chaitanya was working. He met them at his first hotel. He came and sat on a chair.

Mr. Luthra: Is that it? Only 24 people? Anyways. As you know Mr. Chaitanya is no more, and you don't have anyone to help in India. Let me help what you can do and where.

All the 24 criminals explained from where they can buy drugs and sell. There dealers are across all the world. Also, they kidnapped minor girls, give them the drug to look older than twenty-five-year and sold them in other countries.

Mr. Luthra: I will help you with all your businesses. In return I want 25% of the profit.

A Criminal: What? We will not give you that much profit. We have to risk on our lives, give money to police, clear the navy, and then supply here. We will give you the same as Mr. Chaitanya. No more extra.

Mr. Luthra signed Rafiq to open the door. A bunch of Police Officers entered in the room and point a gun on them. They all got panicked.

Mr. Luthra: Relax, boys. You must give me what I want. Otherwise, you know the results.

A criminal: We want sometime to discuss.

Mr. Luthra: This is not a discussion room. This is the discission room. My offer is not negotiable. You have to accept this. Okay, I give all of you two options. Either you accept or leave. As I have another meeting so, you have only two minutes to think.

As soon as criminal stood up from his chair, a police officer shot him. Everyone there got scared.

Mr. Luthra: Anyone. Clock is ticking and I don't have all day. You have only one and half minutes left.

They criminal saw each other face. Mr. Luthra lit the cigar.

A criminal: 20%?

Mr. Luthra: As I said, it is non-negotiable.
A police officer shot him too.
One of the criminals slammed his hand on table as a deal. Seeing him, other criminals also slammed the table to agree on Mr. Luthra. Mr. Luthra stood up.
Mr. Luthra: Okay. I hope we have a great business ahead.
One of the criminals slammed his hand on thigh as a deal. Seeing him, other criminals also slammed on thighs to agree on Mr. Luthra. Everyone slams continuously on thighs. Mr. Luthra evil laughs and stood up.

4.24 - A Date & A Time

Chapter 5

It ends from where it started

4.24 - A Date & A Time

New Delhi. 15th April 2017

Six months has been passed and Mr. Luthra became the 1st Indian richest businessman and in 5th in worldwide. His money and power grow in more than his entire life. He could not handle so much power and became the villain of his own story. He started illegal medicines, drugs, kidnapping and raping minor or major girls. Many people registered a complaint about lost kids, but no one could find them as Mr. Luthra supply them to outer countries. He closed all the files against him with money. He was destroying the world. The same day, he had a conference meeting with all news reporters at his one of a hotel in Delhi. It was in the morning at ten o'clock. Mr. Luthra arrived on time. An event started ordinarily, and host asked reporters to ask their questions.

Reporter: Good morning, Mr. Luthra. I think you get this question most of the time, but as we know you were belonging to poor family and now you are one of the richest persons in the world. How you feel?

Mr. Luthra got angry on reporter.

Mr. Luthra: Stop asking silly question. Weak people remember their past. I live in the future. I feel good, but not great.

Reporter: Why sir? What is bothering you?

Mr. Luthra: Do not interrupt when I am saying something. I will ask you for the next question. So, I want more money. All of them that have in this world. I want to become a king of this world. I'm in 5th position right now and want to be on 1st. I want to

become that one person that no one can ever touch my richness ever.
Reporter: Records are meant to be broken, sir. There are lots of world records that had been broken. This will break too. Maybe not in one year but who knows after ten years.
Mr. Luthra got angry.
Mr. Luthra: No. No one will ever break my richness record. I will be the only person alive.
Mr. Luthra lost his control, got off the stage and caught the reporter's collar. Everyone tried to stop Mr. Luthra but he is totally out of control. Media is taking photos of his behavior.
Mr. Luthra: How can you say this? I will be the only one there. No one will ever be the top of me.
Reporter: Leave me. Leave my collar. Let me go.
Somehow, security managed to control him. They took him backside of the stage. Reporter could not control his anger and shouted.
Reporter: Mr. Luthra. The hunger for money has gone to your head. Control it or you will not know when you will drown. Everyone knows how you reached from top fifty to fifth position. Here we all know about your illegal businesses, black money, direct contact with government, and what not. We just can't publish it because you kill us.
Mr. Luthra: Tell him to shut up.
Reporter: One last question from my side. There are few reporters who publish an article about your illegal businesses in 2012, next day they all died. Police said

that they committed suicide. What about it? Do you have any answer of it?

Mr. Luthra could not hold his anger. He took a gun from his back and shot on reporter's head. Everyone was stunned after seeing this. Media was still taking photos and notes of it. Mr. Luthra's eyes were being red.

Mr. Luthra: If anyone wants to publish an article related to this, you know what it will going to cost you.

Mr. Luthra put a gun behind his back and left for hotel. The other side, the case was cold, and Sanjay let Manoj and Santosh go. Government suspended Manoj to next six months. Manoj, Santosh, and Anaya met at the coffee shop.

Manoj: Shit. We have so much evidence but still we can't do anything about Mr. Luthra. He went so far in just few months.

Anaya: Please don't include this time into the mission. Last time when I was with Yuvika, only I know how I handled the situation.

Manoj: What about her? What is she doing?

Anaya: She started makeup and modeling class at her home. Life isn't that hard that people think.

Manoj: Can we…

Anaya: No. You know that we don't even know where Mr. Luthra stays. He has a house, but he hardly went there. If he found out that we filed a case and Yuvika is the witness, then he will kill us too. She started her new journey and after a long time she is being real in her world.

Manoj: Do your job Anaya. People want change but no one want to change.
Manoj stood up and leave at his car.
Santosh: Don't upset ma'am. He is stressed with work.
Anaya: Yes. I want to change the world but don't want to sacrifice anyone more.
Manoj came again and changed the channel of café TV.
Reporter: Police found Mr. Srinivasan dead in this morning at his home. He killed himself by shot on his head and left a video of his suicide reason.

***

Mr. Srinivasan was sitting on his working chair at his home.
Mr. Srinivasan (In video): Hello everyone. I don't know what to say. I had been working more than thirty years. My goal was not to become rich by money. My goal was to get rich by name. Which I earned too. But from a few weeks, I could not sleep peacefully. I… I got a death threat from someone. Few months ago, he kidnapped my family, my wife, my son, and his wife to get some information from me. Later, he let them go. He took control of my most of the companies and turned them to illegal businesses. He has his own companies, but no one wants to spoil their own name. My goal is to make a happy place for people, and not to spoil their future. My companies donate most of the profit to trusts and poor people. He turned them into money making illegal businesses. He is ruining everyone's life and killing people.
Mr. Srinivasan stood up from his chair, got angry and started shouting.

Mr. Srinivasan (In video): He was the murderer, kidnapper, rapist, drug supplier and God knows what he did. His only want money and power by hook or by crook. He was none other than Mr. Luthra. He was the mastermind to all the businesses. He was the one who forced to suicide Mr. Khanna. My dearest friend, Chintu. Everyone knows Chaitanya is doing illegal businesses, but no one knows under whom. Mr. Luthra asked him to do it.

Mr. Srinivasan started crying.

Mr. Srinivasan (In video): And I know that after this video leak, he will kill me too. But before he kills me, I will kill myself.

He opened the droor and took a gun. He cries continuously.

Mr. Srinivasan (In video): I don't know if this video will reach to the public or not but if it is, then please save the world.

Mr. Srinivasan shot himself on his head and video ended.

***

News shows Mr. Srinivasan's dead body on national TV.

Reporter: After this video, police started searching on Mr. Luthra to arrest him. All states are on high alert. Government orders all the police officers to shot wherever they found Mr. Luthra. Mr. Luthra's all property has been sealed. During this, they found contacts with foreign criminals who supplies drugs to India. Also, they found Mr. Luthra's illegal businesses and relationship with criminals in different cities in all over India. Few of them are shot dead and more to go.

Anaya: Manoj, why don't you know all of this?

Manoj: Because I am suspended. How would I know? There is a one person that can help.

Manoj called Sanjay. The same time Anaya received a call from Yuvika.

Manoj: Jai hind, sir.

Sanjay: Jai hind, Manoj. Thank you for helping us. Remember, you and your friend were in storage? You both found case files against Mr. Luthra, brought the evidence, and I already submit that to high court. Because of that, court ordered to shoot him dead. And congratulations, your suspension will be void soon. Soon you will get letter of re-join duty.

Manoj: Then... Thank you, sir. I don't...

Sanjay: No need to say anything. If you find any clue of Mr. Luthra then you know what to do.

Sanjay hung up the call. Anaya was talking with Yuvika.

Yuvika: Hi, Ana. How are you?

Anaya: I'm too good. How are you? How are things going?

Yuvika: Things are going great. At first, I was so upset but in the end everything is fine. My mother and father are so happy that I am with them most of the time.

Anaya: I told you. When something ends, it means there will be new start. Tell me more about it.

Yuvika: Oh, it's a long story. Can we meet this Saturday?

Anaya: Great. Which bar?

Yuvika: Not in the bar. We'll meet in restaurant. Dinner is on me.
Anaya: Great. Text me the address and I'll be there. Bye.
Anaya hung up the call. She saw Manoj in stressed.
Anaya: What happened? What are you thinking about?
Manoj: Nothing. Who was that?
Anaya: It was Yuvika. But what happened to you? Who was on the call?
Santosh: It was Sanjay sir, and Manoj sir is thinking about Mr. Luthra. Where is he? How to find him? What to do?
Anaya: Come on, Manoj. You tried to find evidence against Mr. Luthra and punished him and this is what is happening. You should be happy.
Manoj: Wait a minute. Yuvika knows the locations of Mr. Luthra. You said she was with him from too long. She definitely knows something about him.
Anaya got a call from Shekhar. He was so tensed and scared.
Shekhar: Hello?
Anaya: Hello, Shekhar. What happened?
Shekhar: Come to the lab. It's urgent.
Anaya: What happened? Hello?
Shekhar hung up the call.
Manoj: What happened?
Anaya: It's Shekhar's call. He was scared. I must go to the lab.
Manoj: Wait, we are coming with you. Santosh, you can go on duty.
Manoj and Anaya both left for the lab.

4.24 - A Date & A Time

**

When they reached there, everything was ruined. All equipment, camera, test tubes were broken. They both shocked after seeing this. Shekhar was sitting on the chair and was slight bleeding from his head.

Anaya: Shekhar? What happened? Are you okay? Who did this? Manoj, pass the med kit.

Shekhar: I don't know. I was performing a test, and someone hit me with the rod. When I woke up, I saw this.

Manoj: But who did this? Do you have any enemy?

Anaya: No. How? Why? I mean why I have an enemy? I didn't do anything that can hurt anyone. I'm just working in the lab and in crime branch. First, let me just help Shekhar.

Manoj got a call from commissioner; he went outside to attend. Shekhar held Anaya's hand, grabbed her closer and said something in his ear. She was shocked and scared. She got a call from Yuvika. Anaya hung up the call, but she received again. Anaya thought maybe it was urgent.

Anaya: Yes, what happened? I'm busy in something.

Yuvika: Oh, sorry to disturb you. There is a change in plan. I am going with my parents in evening. Can we meet in few? Or we can shift it to tomorrow?

Anaya: No... No, it is okay. We can meet right now.

Yuvika: Sure? Aren't you busy?

Anaya: I... I was busy. But we can meet. Anything for you. We will meet at your home if you are okay with it.

Yuvika: Surely, why not. I will send you my house location.

Anaya: Sure. Bye. Manoj? Can you please take care of him? I have to go somewhere else.
Manoj: Sure. Is everything okay? Can I come with you?
Anaya: Yes, everything is okay. It was Yuvika. She… Ladies problem, you know.
Manoj: Okay. Just ask her about Mr. Luthra and call me if you got anything.
Anaya leave from there.
Santosh: Sir, can you please bandage this properly, please?

**

Anaya went at Yuvika's house. She rung the bell and Yuvika opened the door. She wore an Indian suite.
Yuvika: Hey, Ana. After a long time.
Anaya: Hey. You look so different.
Yuvika: Thanks. Come, come.
Anaya: What happened? You look stressed on call. Is everything okay?
Yuvika: I need one favor from you. It is about Mr. Luthra. I was the closest one after his family. I know where he hides himself in this kind of situation. I can't tell the police about it because they will counter question 'How do you know? What is your relationship with him?' I only trust you on this. As you are a lawyer so, you can tell the police about his location. But I will tell you but in one condition.
Anaya: What condition?
Yuvika: Promise me that you will give him worst punishment as possible. He should struggle between life and death. Every day he struggles and beg for his

life. Neither he lives nor dead. He should beg for death, but he should suffer the pain he gave to others.

Anaya was shocked a little after hearing this.

Anaya: I promise.

Yuvika: His one of the best places to hide his villa away from the city if he is Delhi. It was a jungle area, and no one even allowed to walk that way. You require his permission to enter that property over 4KM because it has full protection with fences, guards, and all. Villa was so big and confusing that I almost forgot way.

Anaya: How many times you had been there? And why government did not know about it?

Yuvika: Most of the time when Luthra is in Delhi, we met at his farmhouse only. I know most of the path to enter his villa without permission. But be careful. If they saw you, then they will shoot you on your head. Not even animals allowed in his territory. I don't know why government not aware of this. And yes. He said it was a haunted house and no one ever visit this villa and maybe government declared it to non-visited area.

Anaya: Okay. I'll take care of it. Show me the map and I'll do whatever possible.

Yuvika helped Anaya to route Mr. Luthra's territory. Anaya's mobile rings and it was Manoj.

Manoj: Anaya, we found who destroyed your lab.

Anaya: Who?

Manoj: Aditya and Dhairya. Why they do that? Is there any enmity?

Anaya: I had no idea. But I request you to please arrest them and I wanted to talk. How can some forensic doctor destroy the lab? And why?

Manoj: They will be in my police custody in few minutes. You can come there.
Anaya: Okay. I'll be there.
Anaya hung up the call. Yuvika saw her in tense and stress. Yuvika took water glass and offered her.
Yuvika: Is everything okay?
Anaya: Yes. Yuvika… Thanks for your help. You…
Yuvika: No, Ana. Mr. Luthra should be punished and should be behind bars. He had done…
Yuvika got emotional. Anaya hugged her and left to police station.

**

Anaya arrived in police station and saw Aditya and Dhairya behind bars.
Anaya: Manoj? Can I talk with them for few minutes?
Manoj let Anaya talk with them. She came near to the cell.
Anaya: Why?
Aditya: Jealousy.
Anaya: I never did anything wrong that you feel jealous of me.
Aditya: I was jealous because you buried my reputation, my honor and handling bigger cases, got promoted, medals, name, fame, and what I get? Nothing. In fact, I am behind these bars where you committed crime. Right?
Anaya got scared a little.
Anaya: It is because of your work and behavior. You didn't do anything good that government gave you medals. You are my senior, right? You started work before me. Still you are not capable because work is not

only we have to do. There should be ethics, behavior. Tell me, how many cases you solved? What evidence you submitted to court? The problem is you and not me. If you work honestly than you will receive more than I have. Government will give me new equipment but think about yourself. Your career is ended. Ego ended your career.

Anaya hit his bag on the bar and left to find Mr. Luthra.

Manoj: Hey, Anaya.

Anaya: Yes, what happened?

Manoj: Have you asked Yuvika about Mr. Luthra's location?

Anaya: Yes, but she didn't know anything about it. I think police department have to find themselves.

**

She left the police station and went at the same location Yuvika said, but there was no road to enter in the jungle. She started investigating and found two guards with guns roaming in the jungle. She was on the right path. Anaya started following them but unluckily, guards heard someone following them. Anaya was scared and somehow managed to escape. She started following them in day and night till she finds the Mr. Luthra's villa's safe entry.

**

The other side, Mr. Luthra was sitting on sofa with Rafiq drinking alcohol and watching news where everyone was looking for him to kill. He was so frustrated, and angry.

Mr. Luthra: Rafiq, It's all over. I have nothing to do for now. I don't know what to do. All the things that I earned was shattered, broke like a glass.

Rafiq (Sign language): No worry. We are safe here. No one will ever touch you or catch you.

Mr. Luthra: I know. But, how long I stay here? I want to live a normal life like before. It is all because that Mr. Srinivasan.

Mr. Luthra grabbed the bottle of alcohol and dink it from bottle. Rafiq tried to stop him by snatching bottle.

Mr. Luthra: Let me drink. I want to end Mr. Srinivasan's all businesses like he did mine. He died but he should cry from heaven. It was my mistake that I left him that day. I should end his whole family.

Mr. Luthra tried to snatch a bottle from Rafiq.

Rafiq (Sign language): No. Stop behaving like that. Time will change again, and you will be free in some months. You will again roam freely with your family.

Mr. Luthra: No, Rafiq. Okay. One last thing I want. Then I will do whatever you say, okay?

Rafiq: Okay. What do you want?

Mr. Luthra: I want that drug to feel my power again. I will take it only one and this will be my last time. And remember, you said Mr. Srinivasan had granddaughter? I want her here. This is my last wish, Rafiq. Please fulfil it.

Mr. Luthra was so drunk that he unconscious after that. Rafiq was too loyal to Mr. Luthra that he can do anything for his master. In just a week, his people in Chennai kidnapped Mr. Srinivasan's granddaughter and transport to Mr. Luthra's villa via ship. Rafiq gave him a one tablet of steroid and put other in a droor in the room.

Rafiq (Sign language): Only one, no more. You age, body and health won't handle more than one so please do not overdose.

Mr. Luthra got angry.

Mr. Luthra: Don't tell me what to do. I know what is good for me. You are just my servant so, behave like a servant. Bring one more whiskey with some ice cube and get lost.

Rafiq didn't like this behavior of Mr. Luthra. He left angrily.

New Delhi. 22nd April 2017

A week has been past and still police could not find Mr. Luthra's location. Anaya knows everything but she didn't tell anyone about it. The other side, Manoj asked question on Aditya and Dhairya in Investigation room.
Manoj: I don't have much time so please do it fast. Why?
Aditya: Because we found that murderer.
Manoj: What? You were not jealous of Anaya?
Aditya: No. I was just messing with her. We didn't want any major case who explode our mind. We both always come in time and chill in the lab with minor cases, and we are very happy with our government job and benefits.
Manoj: Then why you destroy the lab?
Aditya: Actually, we went there, and Shekhar was working on something. I told him we need evidence that they found in Mr. Bose, and that politicians to examine and match with Mr. Chaitanya's evidence. But he refused and we don't like who interfere in our work.
Dhairya: Yes, and we all had a minor fight in which we broke a flask and some glass tubes nothing else. I pushed Shekhar to a glass, and he bleeds from head.
Manoj: You broke the law. It is crime and he can file a case against you to hit him or try to murder. You know how sensitive it is?
Aditya: We know the law too, sir. He didn't have any proof that we tried to kill him.
Manoj: The stitches, blood, your fingerprint and CCTV footage shows everything, Aditya.

4.24 - A Date & A Time

Dhairya took Manoj's hand and place on his wrist.

Dhairya: Now, if I went outside and scratched a little bit here, it means you scratched it, right? Can I file a harassment case against you? Can I file a complaint for a police officer harm a person behind the bars until he got notice from court.

Manoj: This is not how it works.

Aditya: That is what we were explaining from last few minutes. We had a minor fight doesn't mean we tried to murder him.

Manoj: Okay. What about evidence? Did you get anything.

Dhairya: I was examining on it. If you give me few more minutes, then I will tell you who is the murderer.

Manoj: What do you suspect?

Aditya: If I say the name, you won't believe it. You will shout like a Bollywood movie; 'What? No, tell me this is wrong. She will never do this.'

Dhairya: And we give you false consolation; 'Believe it, Manoj. She is the one who betrayed us. She was the murderer, Manoj.'

Dhairya started acting like crying. Aditya laughed on it.

Manoj: Stop it. Do you think this is any kind of joke?

Aditya: This isn't, Manoj. But...

Manoj: Who is he?

Dhairya: You need to concentrate on your listening skill. We said 'She'. A person who murdered Mr. Bose and all was a woman, and she is roaming freely outside.

Manoj: Who is she?

Aditya: Your friend, Anaya Kadri.

Manoj: What?

Aditya: Honestly, I wanted to take revenge of my job, my work, my reputation by replacing evidence with Anaya sample. Guess what, I didn't have to. And I am hundred percent confident that Shekhar knows about it. That is why he was resisting to take past evidence.
Manoj: No. It can't be her. She was…
Dhairya: There it is. I told you that dialogue earlier.
Manoj: Shut up. Do you know what you are saying? I know her very well. She is not that kind of person. Do you have any proof or evidence?
Aditya: We have everything you need to know, Manoj. Just take us to our lab and we will help you to solve this case.
Manoj: I don't believe you two. You both are lying. If I take you outside, you both will run away.
Aditya: I told you, Manoj. We know the law.
Manoj stood up and about to leave from the room.
Aditya: I know you won't believe us and take us back to lab for evidence. Unless, Anaya is your friend, right? You can't tolerate someone accusing her. But this is the truth, Manoj. You must face it. Either now or after Mr. Luthra's death.
Manoj shocked and stopped.
Manoj: Where did he come from?
Dhairya: Murderer killed only those people who were working or close to Mr. Luthra.
Manoj: I already know that. What is the connection between Mr. Luthra and Anaya?
Aditya: All the murders were done by Anaya Kadri. When we came from Mr. Chaitanya's crime scene with evidence, we found a small piece of cloth from bed.

Dhairya: It is a same perfume that Anaya used most of the time. I am telling you; it is gross. Yuck.

Aditya: Then, we went to Anaya's lab and gently asked Shekhar for Mr. Bose, Mr. Jain, and Mr. Sisodia clues.

Dhariya: He ignored that and didn't gave us. Then we forced him for that.

Aditya: It was not aggressive or fighting or blood etc. what you are thinking. We took evidence and already gave it to our team. Soon, you will receive the report in which mention that 'Anaya and clues received at murder places are MATCHED'.

Dhariya: Then, it will be your call what to do.

Manoj got curious. She didn't kill Mr. Chaitanya but her fingerprint, blood, and other evidence shows that she killed him.

Manoj: No. That can't be true.

Aditya: This is true. Take us to the lab and we will prove it. We took previous evidence from her lab, and it will surely match. Not only Mr. Chaitanya, but she also killed Mr. Bose…

Manoj: If it is a lie, then…

Dhairya: Your gun and our head. Just shoot straight down the middle of our head. We can also give it in writing. Or you can make it like an encounter.

Manoj: Santosh, take him to the lab. Ask team to find Shekhar and take him to police station.

**

Manoj, Shekhar, Aditya, and Dhairya went to the lab. Dhairya started examining the evidence.

Dhairya: All the evidence placed for a match. It will take few hours to get results. Till then, let's order something. I am so hungry. What will you eat?
Manoj: How much time it will take?
Dhairya: Around 1-2 hours for all. And what will you eat?
Manoj: I don't want anything. I just want results.
Santosh: Sir, team brought Shekhar to police station.
Manoj: Okay. Tell them to keep an eye on him. We'll be there after ending this case.

**

Anaya: Ammi, I am going for work.
Fatima arrived and kissed on her forehead.
Fatima: Don't worry. Allah will always protect you and give justice.
Anaya: And…
Fatima: Yes, I know. I will not wait for you for lunch or dinner and take medicine. Khuda hafiz.

**

After a few hours, results came. It was 23rd April 2017 in midnight. All the evidence matches with Anaya's. The finger tissues on a rope where they found at Mr. Bose's, Hair sample, which is different from Kavya. Mr. Jain and Mr. Sisodia blood and collided Anaya's blood with them. Fingerprint, tissues, and more in Mr. Chaitanya's body was also matched with Anaya. Manoj and Santosh both were shocked after seeing this report.
Manoj: I don't believe it. How? Why?
Aditya: We already told you that it was Anaya who killed all of them. The question is 'Why?'

Dhairya: So, Mr. Manoj. Now, we are free to go, and your mission is to catch and punish Anaya.

Manoj: You will free and when I say. Santosh, put them in the van and bring them police station.

They all left with the reports to a police station.

**

Shekhar was sitting on a bench waiting Manoj.

Shekhar: What happened, sir? Why they arrest me like this? What have I done?

Manoj: Santosh, bring him to the room.

Santosh grabbed Shekhar's hand and took him to interrogation room. He was confused why they were treating like a criminal. Manoj slammed reports Infront of him.

Manoj: From how long you know Anaya?

Shekhar: From college. She was my junior and after college, she became my senior. We never talked in college but knew that there is some Anaya in college because she always tops in class.

Manoj: What else do you about her?

Shekhar: Not more about her family. She only has a mother She never mentioned about her father.

Manoj: During postmortem, did she ever hand a knife like she was killing someone?

Shekhar: What? No. We all practice holding a knife and handle it like a pen. We are working with each other from more than two years, and I never saw her like this.

Manoj: This report says she killed Mr. Bose, Mr. Jain, Mr. Sisodia and Mr. Chaitanya.

Shekhar: She only didn't kill Mr. Chaitanya. You were the one who killed Mr. Chaitanya. You took your father's revenge, right?

Manoj: What does it mean? How do you?

Manoj was confused after Shekhar's statement. Shekhar looked in his eyes fearlessly.

Shekhar: You directly asked questions to other criminals. But you didn't ask me directly. You go round and round and round. Your question should be 'Is this report true?' And I will say 'Yes.' Anaya was the one who killed all of them. Mr. Bose, Mr. Jain, Mr. Sisodia, Mr. Chaitanya, and in few hours, Mr. Luthra, You cannot stop her until she wants to. She is on a mission. She is on revenge.

Manoj: What revenge? She can't take the law in hand. She will get punish for this. You were with her from the start, right? You knew about from very long. You lied about it. She will be in big trouble. Where is she? Where is she right now?

Shekhar: I told you the truth. You took your revenge to kill Mr. Chaitanya. You took law in your hands, then why you are not wrong? You ran from there, save yourself. In the same case, Anaya is doing the same thing. She is taking her revenge, and she is wrong. Honestly, I don't know what it is about, but she is right whatever she is doing. I don't know where she is and what she will do, but she will kill Mr. Luthra at any cost.

Manoj: You know nothing then how can be so sure that she is right? How will I trust you on this? Don't make me to torture you to say the truth.

Shekhar: Don't use your energy on me. I said whatever I know. I saw trust and believed in her mother's eyes. She just said 'Shekhar, take care of Anaya. She is not responsible whatever she is doing'. She told this to Anaya several times.

Manoj: What does that mean? Who is responsible?

Shekhar: Don't know. Neither we asked, nor she said.

Manoj: She will say. Santosh. Bring Anaya's mother here. And what about Mr. Luthra? Did we get anything?

Santosh: No, sir. All region is looking for him.

Manoj: Before Anaya kills hm and create any blunder, we must save her as well as kill Mr. Luthra.

Shekhar: Try but you can't. Anaya will surrender after her mission is complete. You don't have to find her in every state like a criminal. She will explain how, why, and when killed each and everyone.

Manoj shouted by an anger.

Manoj: Santosh. Bring Anaya's mother, right now.

**

Santosh went to Anaya's house and arrest Anaya's mother. She was not shocked as she knows the day will come when police arrest her.

Manoj: Hello, ma'am. Please sit. I… I w…. Why is Anaya killing all those people?

Fatima: Why you kill Mr. Chaitanya?

Manoj: I'm sorry ma'am but, you are not in a stage to counter question. Right now, you are a relative of a criminal which helping her to do crime. I can put you in the cell to helping her. I only want to know why, where, and when.

Fatima: I'm asking because the reason is the same. You took revenge of your father's death. She was doing the same thing. Her…

Manoj: I have only few questions that I want you to answer without any philosophy. Who was his father? What is this revenge about? And where is she now?

Fatima: You don't have much time to listen my answers. I can only say that her father's name is Mohammad Faizal Kadri. He has a saree store in Delhi. He loves his children so much that he…

Fatima got emotional and started crying. Manoj offered her a glass of water.

Manoj: Children? Anaya never mentioned about her sister. How many kids do you have?

Fatima: Two. Anaya was my second daughter. My first daughter named was Inayat. Like her name meaning, she was so kind and caring. She died at the age of sixteen. She died Infront of Anaya. They both were just kids.

Fatima again started crying.

Fatima: You can't think how it looks like when your loved ones died Infront of you and you can't do anything. No one supported us that time and no one help us to give justice. Her father run for court, police, judge but no one help us. We wanted to punish who killed Inayat at any cost. I prayed God to give us justice. Then came Anaya to take revenge of her sister's death. Anaya name meaning is God's answer, and she proved it. She took revenge of her sister's death revenge at the age of fourteen only.

Fatima was sobbing. Manoj hugged her tightly.

Manoj: Shush. I'm sorry. I know how it feels like to lose someone. My father died Infront of me. He was in police department and gangsters shot him Infront of me. I remember when he took his last breath in my hand. I was kid too that time, I couldn't do anything. It was Mr. Chaitanya who sent gangsters to kill my father.

Unfortunately, Santosh came to the room, and he was panic.

Santosh: Manoj sir, a girl… A girl kidnapped again. She is also a teenager of about sixteen years old.

Manoj: It has to be Mr. Luthra. We must find her soon. Hopefully, Anaya will be at the same location.

Manoj was about to leave for the research, suddenly he realized something.

Manoj: Wait a minute. Anaya met Yuvika last time. Try to track Anaya mobile number. I know she might turn off her mobile number and left somewhere else but tried it once. Call Yuvika and get Mr. Luthra's location.

Santosh: Why Yuvika? Don't you want to know who is that girl?

Manoj: Who is she?

Santosh: Mr. Srinivasan's granddaughter. He kidnapped her.

Manoj: He is taking revenge by raping her and surely later killed her. Get Yuvika' s number and I'll talk to her. She definitely knew something about it.

Santosh tried to track Anaya's location with the help of her mobile, but it showed at her own house.

Manoj: I knew about it. Have you got Yuvika' s number?

Santosh: Yes, sir.

Santosh finds Yuvika's number and calls her and handed over.

Yuvika: Hello?

Manoj: Hello, Is this Ms. Yuvika?

Yuvika: Yes. May I know who is this?

Manoj: This is Inspector Manoj. I am working with Anaya Kadri. She informed us that you gave her Mr. Luthra's location, and we were tracking but her signal lost. We wanted to know Mr. Luthra's location. Where is he right now?

Yuvika: She went to that place. But why? She is a lawyer and she… Why?

Manoj: Yuvika, just tell us the location of him so we can catch him. Anaya already told us about everything. Trust me, we won't involve you in this. We are here to help. She will get hurt if Mr. Luthra caught him.

Yuvika hung up without saying anything. Manoj finds strange and loss hope. His mobile rings. Yuvika sent a location in a jungle.

Manoj: Santosh, get ready with team. We were heading to kill Mr. Luthra and save that girl and Anaya.

**

Manoj and his team headed to Mr. Luthra's villa. They went to near and see fences.

Manoj: Yuvika said that there will be so many guards to protect the villa and it will be almost 4KM inside it. Santosh, tell the team to not to enter with vehicle and divide them to find the location. If they see anyone else in the jungle, they have right to kill them. Try not to make any noise. Let see how much kill we got today.

Santosh informed the team, and they all went in the jungle.

Manoj went with four more people in jungle and found few guards in their way. They took gun in pocket and went to hand-to-hand combat. Somehow, they managed to find villa center of the jungle.

**

Rafiq brought Mr. Srinivasan's granddaughter to Mr. Luthra. She was unconscious. Mr. Luthra slapped Rafiq.

Mr. Luthra: Why is she unconscious? I am a man. I don't take advantage of the girl being unconscious. Wake her up and then I'll start my program.

Rafiq got so angry and left from there without saying anything. Mr. Luthra didn't try to stop him. After a few hours, she awakes and saw someone was taking drug. Mr. Luthra saw her.

Mr. Luthra: Hello, darling. You awake.

Shruti: What? My head. Where am I?

Mr. Luthra: You are in Delhi in my villa. Don't worry, you are safe.

Shruti was starting afraid.

Shruti: How… How I get it? Who are you?

Mr. Luthra: You don't know me? That hurts, darling. I am the richest, wealthiest, powerful businessman Mr. Luthra. You can call me darling. My people brought you here.

Shruti: But why? What do you want?

Mr. Luthra took five tablets of steroids at once.

Mr. Luthra: I was stuck in this villa from long time, and no one came here to pleasure me. That is why they

brought you to entertain me. As specially, because of your grandfather I stuck here. He took everything from me. My money, power, family, everything. So, in return, I want your virginity.
Shruti started screaming for help.
Mr. Luthra: No, no. It won't help. No one can listen and come here. This place is far away from city as well as highway. Just give me what I want and as long as I want, then I'll let you go. In fact, the same people will drop you at home. Now, come to me.
Mr. Luthra became so aggressive. He grabbed her shoulder, tried to kiss on neck and started tearing her clothes. She was screaming, tried to push him but he was so strong. Somehow, she managed to run from there. She was screaming so loud and asking for help. But the place was so far from the city that no one could hear her voice. Her clothes were torn from chest, thighs, and shoulders. She was having so many scratches on her body and blood was coming. Her eyes were red, and her body was shaking.
Mr. Luthra: Come on. Why are you running from me? There is nowhere you can go. I bought this big farmhouse just for us. Don't run so much. I am too old anyway for this. You are making me use all my energy in running. What will we do on bed? Huh?
She arrived at the door and starts knocking it, but it was closed from outside. She continuous screamed for help.
Shruti: No. Please, help. Somebody, open the door. Please let me out. Is somebody out there? Please help, open it. I want to go.

4.24 - A Date & A Time

She was breathing heavily, crying for help, unfortunately, nobody was there to listen. Mr. Luthra came after her. He felt breathlessness. He took a deep breath, crack his back a little and started walking towards her.

Mr. Luthra: As I told you darling, nobody is here. To hear your scream. I am not going to hurt you. Although, I will give you lots of money to enjoy your life. In return, all I want is your virginity. At first, it hurts but it is a lot of fun later.

He forcibly grabbed her hand and starts pounding her. She was trying extremely hard to stop him but, she was not strong enough to resist. Mr. Luthra slammed her at door, turned over forcibly and started ripping off her clothes again.

Shruti: Please, stop. I am just sixteen. Let me go.

Mr. Luthra: Oh, stop shouting. Just enjoy it. I know you are just sixteen, that is why I want you. I am not going to hurt you, darling. Just a few minutes and you will be holy.

Suddenly, he heard someone walking and smells of a dirty sock. As soon as he turned around to look, someone cut his throat slightly. He was wearing a formal black suit, and his entire face is covered with a black mask. Mr. Luthra not able to speak anything, but he is alive. He fell on the ground. That person saw a girl crying and pointed at room, as telling her to leave from there. She grabbed her torn clothes from ground and run towards the room without looking back and what that person will do with Mr. Luthra. There were paintings on the wall and a flowerpot with fake flowers on the table. Mr. Luthra grabbed those things and started throwing them at people. That person first dodged and strongly grabbed his left hand to again make a long cut on his forearms. He started crying and trying to speak but could not. His right hand is on his throat which is stopping blood and left hand is pouring blood continuously which he can't stop. Because of the cut, his second hand loses sensation and muscles being weak. After a few minutes, his left arm became paralyzed. A person is standing there without saying a word or any other intense movement. Mr. Luthra tried to open the door, but it was locked from the outside. He starts running away from him. Again, that person stabbed the knee of left leg. It was so intense that his leg was paralyzed too in no time. That person did not get closer to Mr. Luthra till that time. When all this was done, he opened the droor and found magazines and newspapers which had his photo on the front page. The person tore only those pages that contained his face and spread all around. Mr. Luthra tries to fold his hands and begs for his life. Person was waiting until all the blood comes out from his body and die.

A person removed the mask, she was Anaya.

Anaya: Now you see, how it looks like to brutally kill someone. I can kill you the same way as you killed my sister fifteen-years ago. But I am not like you who insert a wooden stick inside of someone after rape. Remember this date? The same date, the same time, in Delhi fifteen years ago. Remember, you entered a house drunk. A father woke up and you and your friend Garge hit him with wase, then a mother came.

4.24 - A Date & A Time

You hit her too to make unconscious. Me and my sister INAYAT, both woke up after hearing noises. You enter a children's room where you thought we were sleeping but we hide from you. My sister tried to hit you with a wooden stick on your head. But you both counterattack her. Garge grabbed her both hand, you grabbed her leg, torn the clothes, made her naked and raped. Remember? I was hide in the vault door. I was seeing all of this when I was a kid. I want to save my sister but didn't have guts to get out from there. I was afraid if you done the same with me. After a few minutes you ended, and Garge started raping her. After a few minutes when he finished, you both didn't stop there. You took the same wooden stick and put it inside her, remember? First, you raped her and then brutally killed her. You murdered an innocent child. I hope I can give you the same pain my sister had. But I am not like you, a rapist. Look at you.

Blood from Mr. Bose's neck, hand and leg continuous. He tried to joint both hands and asked for forgiveness. Anaya: What? Oh, you are bagging for your life, struggling between life and death. You want to either die or live, but you can't do anything. Once, my sister was struggling in the same era, but with more pain. Your death is the justice for my sister.

Blood flow was too much and in no time, Mr. Luthra died. The time was 4:24 in the morning on the date of 24th April. It was the same date, and time when Anaya's sister Inayat died.

Anaya: Inayat Di. Your justice has been served. I am sorry I could not save you that day. I think if I saved you that day then life would be different.

This whole incident took only 20 minutes. After his death, Anaya again put mask on to get out from the crime scene. Suddenly, she heard police siren, and she stopped. Manoj opened the door and saw Mr. Luthra dead, and that person was standing there. Manoj and his team pointed guns at murderer and asked to remove mask and surrender. Anaya removed the mask, and everybody was shocked.

Manoj: Anaya? Is that you? They were right. You murdered all those people.

Anaya sat on her knees and put her hand behind her head without saying anything. Her revenge was taken, and she wanted to surrender as her mother said. Manoj and his team handcuff Anaya and brought to her for interrogation in police station.

**

Manoj entered the room where Anaya was sitting with handcuff. She was constantly looking into Manoj's an eye.

Manoj: Why?

Anaya stared to Manoj for a few minutes.

Anaya: To give my sister justice. In 2002, when I was fifteen years old, Mr. Luthra and his friend Garge came to our house drunk around four o'clock. We never saw them, or my father doesn't have any enemy. They came, hit my parents, raped my sister, kill her, and then leave like it was a normal thing for them. The whole incidence took Infront of my eyes. I can't forget that date and time. My father was struggling to give justice and punish Mr. Luthra and Garge, but he failed, the system failed. We didn't have much money to bribe, but they had. Case was closed. My parents were crying, Ammi praying Allah to give justice to us, but nothing happened.

Anaya's eyes filled with tears, but he fearlessly continuous.

Anaya: One day when I was going to school, I saw Garge on a street roaming freely and teasing school and college girls. He was teasing minor girls by touching on the back, hold hand and pull towards him, kissed them on cheeks. I couldn't handle and throw a stone on his face. It bleeds to his forehead, and I was smiling after seeing this. He saw me and run towards me. I managed to escape but he was too fast. He grabbed my hair and started slapping me. I thought he would do the same that he did to Inayat Di. I kicked on his balls; it hurts a lot. I ran again and went to abandon under construction building which was his own. I ran to sixth floor. I went to an edge. He saw me angrily and started running towards me. I managed to dodge him, his leg slipped, and he fell from sixth floor. Luckily a rope got caught on his left leg and swung on the fifth floor. I saw him crying and begging for help. He was saying 'Please, save me. I don't want to die.' I saw a rope tied to a column. I went there and…

Manoj: And? You did what?

Anaya: I untied it. I killed him. I took Inayat Di's revenge at the age of fifteen. I looked at the sky and it was so shiny. It was like Inayat Di was happy.

Manoj: You killed a person at the age of fifteen. Why hadn't police arrested you? Why were you alone? What was your parents said? What happened to Garge?
Anaya: I didn't stop there, actually. When I went on ground floor, he was alive and struggling between life and death. Blood was flowing so fast from behind his head. He was breathing so hard, and he looked at me with hope in his eyes. Like he was bagging to me for life again. I thought to save him, but…
Manoj: But?
Anaya: You know we celebrate Eid where we kill a goat? I celebrate Eid that day. I saw a knife in his pocket, and I cut his throat like we kill a goat. Slowly, slowly.
Manoj was stunned after hearing this. He started sweating.
Manoj: You were only fifteen by that time. Has anybody shown you doing this? Why hadn't police arrested you?
Anaya: I cut his head just like cutting a goat, packed in my school bag, and went at home. My bag was bloody, my parents were shocked seeing this. They were asking 'What is this? What happened?' I opened the bag and show them the head of Garge. They were shocked and Ammi was unconscious. They both shocked, scared, cried, and stressed about it. Abbu pushed it away. Then I said, "Ammi, Abbu. You both were struggling to give justice to Inayat Di. But we failed. No one helped us. Ammi, you said we have to fight for truth, right? I gave Inayat Di justice, Ammi. I saw at the sky, and she was smiling." Don't know how police arrived at home and

show Garge's head on floor. No one can doubt on a teenage girl so, they thought Abbu killed him and they took Abbu to police station. The police took him to the court. The court also convicted him guilty after seeing all the evidence and sentenced him to life imprisonment. He didn't even say that I had committed the murder. In fact, whose parents say that their daughter is a murderer. He served the punishment for the crime that I had committed. I was ashamed of myself. I am the worst child ever.

Anaya started crying. Manoj wanted to help her as a friend, but now she was not a friend. She was a criminal who killed four named businessmen.

Manoj: Why hadn't you accepted before that you made the crime? Why hadn't you accepted that you killed all those people?

Anaya: I wanted to, when I did my first murder. I wanted to say that the murder was done by me and not my father. But Ammi told me not to commit as the justice to Inayat Di was not served. Ammi told me to study forensic so that I can learn how forensic doctors examine body, each and every single detail that can harm a person, kill a person without even getting caught. For the past few years, I was examining, practicing on dead bodies and some of them were killed by me too who were rapists. I was getting ready to take my sister's revenge and give her justice. Now, I am accepting that all those murders were done by me. I killed Mr. Bose, Mr. Jain, Mr. Sisodia, and Mr. Luthra. I murder Garge at the age of fifteen. Please arrest me to kill of those people.

Manoj: Have you thought what will happen after this? Court will sentence death. Your mother will live alone rest of her life.

Anaya: Don't worry, Manoj. If you ask her how she feels about it, then she will say nothing. She knew that this day would come one day.

Manoj: What about your father? Have you thought of it?

Anaya got emotional a little.

Anaya: He committed suicide only a few months after going to jail. He felt that he could not settle his daughter, and it was his fault. He was in guilt, in pain. That is why Ammi always says that you are not responsible for anything happening in your life. Garge and Mr. Luthra made me do it. I was not on a list to do such things. Murders, Forensic, and all. Also, people say that 'Everything is written' so these are.

Manoj: Why you killed others? Because they were raping or anything personal?

Anaya: Both reasons. I killed Garge and Mr. Luthra because they were trying to rape girls, and they raped and brutally murdered Inayat Di. I killed Mr. Bose because he trying to rape Kavya. I saved her from the thing that happened to Inayat Di. I could not saw another girl raped and murder. Mr. Khanna didn't remember me, but he was my Abbu's old friend. Before he met Mr. Luthra, Mr. Khanna helped Abbu to give justice. But money is power. Mr. Khanna lay down for money. He confessed all to you and helped to close Mr. Luthra's businesses. He died from fear. Once, Mr. Jain and Mr. Sisodia were also teasing me and Inayat Di when we were just kids. I tried to save Akanksha, but I got there late. They both raped and murdered her already. We had a fight and unluckily, I left evidence there. Because of that Aditya and Dhairya caught me. I heard your story from Santosh. He told me about your wife. I am so sorry about that. I investigated your past too and found out about Mr. Chaitanya. He was not on my list, but I helped you to take your father's revenge and give justice. He will be happy too.

Manoj: Anaya, I… I don't know what to say.

Anaya: Don't say anything, Manoj. I know what will happen and I am ready for it. My Ammi and Shekhar ready for this. I confess in full consciousness that all those murders were committed by me, and no one had helped me to do it. And I am ready for any punishment that the court will give.

Manoj left from there.

**

Manoj made a file with all evidence and Anaya's confession.

**

Few months later, she presented in the court where accepted all the allegations and court sentenced her to death.

*****

There are so many girls who are facing or faced such kind of issues. Most of girls or women has been teased or raped by known or unknown. When they leave from their home for school, college or work, some people starring at them or tease them in public. Still, we as a people won't help them.

It is not their fault who would be roaming around with her whole body covered or wearing short clothes or traditional or diapers. As per law, people have rights to roam and live life they want and stay happy. But this law can be withdrawn Infront of money.

Rapists won't see age, clothes, religion, known-unknown. Some rapists won't satisfy after rape, and they torture and kill the victim. Or sometimes they were scared after raping. Scared that if victim filed a complaint, then their life will be ruined and kills them maybe in pieces.

But what about victim? Sometimes, their own family members questioned them. Society will pity on them, hundreds of answers will have to be given to society, whether boy will accept for marriage or not, fear will always haunt her.

Some of victim parents in small villages or in fear never files a case because of the fear of society. Then the rapists get more power to commit another rape on another girl or woman or a child.

The story is complete fiction but wish this can be true. Anaya Kadri was true. Who can give Justice to thousands of rape victims. Wish someone have that courage who can fight against law for Justice. If Anaya can be real, then maybe Nirbhaya rape case will not happened or didn't took 8 years to Justice. Suryanelli, Shakti mills and Priyanka Reddy rape case can be resolved.

If this thing can be true, then maybe Kolkata rape case won't happen.

www.ingramcontent.com/pod-product-compliance
Lightning Source LLC
LaVergne TN
LVHW041709070526
838199LV00045B/1276